THE PHILOSOPHY RESISTANCE SQUAD

THE PHILOSOPHY RESISTANCE SQUAD

ROBERT GRANT

Little Island

THE PHILOSOPHY RESISTANCE SQUAD
First published in 2021 by
Little Island Books
7 Kenilworth Park
Dublin 6W
Ireland

First published in the USA by Little Island Books in 2022

ISBN: 978-1-912417-30-8

Cover design by Ailsa Cullen
Cover illustration © George Ermos, 2021, licensed exclusively by The Bright Agency: www.thebrightagency.com
Typeset and design by Nolan Book Design
Edited by Síne Quinn
Proofread by Emma Dunne

Printed in Poland by Drukarnia Skleniarz

Little Island receives financial support from the Arts Council / An Chomhairle Ealaíon

10 9 8 7 6 5 4 3 2

For Mam, Dad, Stephen and Andrew

Chapter 1

When one with honeyed words but evil mind
Persuades the mob, great woes befall the state.
— Euripides

Milo Moloney tumbled out of the back seat of the car the instant his dad squealed it to a halt. The Moloneys were cutting it close and were in danger of being late for the opening ceremony. That was the last thing they wanted. Milo's mam, flustered and red-faced, jumped out after him as the three headed for the campus gates. Unmistakable sounds of celebration could be heard bubbling in the distance.

As they reached the gates, they were greeted by a flying drone-ball. Like a tiny spherical helicopter, it whizzed down and floated in mid-air beside them, announcing: 'Welcome, Moloney family. Orientation begins in three minutes. Do not delay.'

'Wow!' said Milo's dad. 'Brilliant.'

They scurried up the tree-lined avenue, as if they wished to run but did not dare.

'For heaven's sake, Milo,' said his mam, catching up to him. Milo was tucking in his shirt with one hand as he jogged and fixing his tie with the other. His school bag hung off his shoulder, and his brand-new blazer trailed along behind him like some limp animal tail. 'You're in an absolute state! Come here and I'll fix you!'

'I'm grand!' said Milo, hiking up his trousers.

His mam licked her thumb to flatten his shaggy brown hair. 'And put on your blazer!'

The school they were headed for was the most famous, the most highly ranked and the wealthiest school in all of Ireland: the Secondary Training Institute for Lifelong Employment, known simply as 'the Institute'. It was the pride and joy of the nation, renowned across the globe for its futuristic, hi-tech campus and the unparalleled excellence of its graduates. Its status was near mythical. Tourists would snap selfies in front of the iconic logo. Visiting world leaders would hold meetings in the board room. Famous film directors would shoot scenes there. Regular folk would take Sunday drives just to see the grounds and to purchase a keepsake from the school's shop.

And somehow, the young, messy, easily distracted Milo Moloney had been accepted here. He was a smart kid – he and his parents knew that – but they were still amazed that he'd managed to focus enough to get in.

The family broke into a full run as they neared the top of the avenue. There were expansive green lawns on either side, the grass as smooth as carpet, like each blade was individually cut with a tiny pair of scissors.

'Put on your blazer!' Milo's mam insisted.

'It's roasting,' Milo protested.

'Milo, not now, please. Just do as you are told.' She hoisted his jacket up around his shoulders. 'I don't want another argument.'

That morning they'd already argued about what to have for breakfast, daily showering and whether you could be sure the world still existed when you shut your eyes.

Just then, the world-famous campus appeared before them like a vision from the distant future. Set into the undulating hills of west Waterford, the campus was made up of a complex of five large white rectangular buildings connected by sleek curved-glass tunnels to a central tower-block. It looked more like an inter-galactic space station than an Irish secondary school. Every detail was smooth and new. And yet it looked like it had always been there. Like the hills were made afterwards as a backdrop for it.

Milo looked up at the coloured laser lights that shone from the rooftops, as if searching for extra-terrestrial life. Several drone-balls whizzed overhead like a swarm of robot bees, carrying signs reading *Welcome First-Years!* Every so often, one would buzz down and snap a photo of a family underneath the famous sign. And there it was, briefly stopping the Moloneys in their tracks, the school's name and motto in bright-blue letters:

Secondary Training Institute for Lifelong Employment
Efficiency in Education

The Moloneys stood under the logo and looked up. It was a special moment for them. Money was tight, but since Milo had been accepted to the Institute, everything had changed. Milo's future was full of possibilities and he was ready for the challenge. He'd never felt so determined before in his whole life.

They made a quick dash for the main entrance, stumbled into the lobby and were met by a group of statue-stiff sixth-year students in a tight semi-circle. The boys and girls stood straight as arrows, with serious faces, wearing immaculate burgundy and grey uniforms. The glowing green school crest indicated they were the prefects – regarded as national heroes. Milo had heard so much about them, how brainy, bright and gifted they were.

Suddenly the prefects marched directly towards him. For a split second, Milo was unnerved by their expressions. They all stared in his direction, but not quite *at* him, more *through* him.

They stopped dead, inches away, towered over him and spoke: 'Mr and Mrs Moloney, welcome to the Secondary Training Institute for Lifelong Employment. Congratulations on your amazing achievement.' They spoke in perfect unison while looking down on Milo. 'Welcome, Milo. This is the first day of the rest of your life. The Institute is the greatest school in the world and you are lucky to be here.'

They saluted, stepped back and all stared in Milo's direction as if he was transparent.

'Look at how disciplined they are,' Milo's mam whispered. 'They are so impressive up close.'

'Now, *that* is how to wear a uniform,' said his dad, nudging Milo.

Milo nodded and tried to meet the students' gaze, but he couldn't shake that unsettled feeling.

'That will be you in a few years,' his dad said.

4

'Ha, yeah, maybe,' Milo answered.

'Please proceed,' one of the prefects said, as they entered a huge circular lobby in the central tower, with ringed balconies ascending several floors, up towards an expansive glass ceiling showing the clear blue sky.

A flash came from one of the drone-balls floating near-by. The ball issued each of them with a biometric smart-strap that automatically clamped to their wrists. It had their photo on it and a red flashing message: *Please make your way to the convention hall.*

'Milo, they have thought of everything!' Mary Moloney said. 'Now, where is the convention hall?'

Then a voice said: 'Please hold the railing.'

The floor began to move, jolting them off balance. It was a travellator, much like one you'd see at the airport. Only this travellator was part of the floor itself.

The travellator moved through the lobby and began to lift into the air. It swung up alongside the ringed balconies as it swirled towards the sky.

'From now on, I refuse to use stairs,' said Milo, laughing. On the fourth floor, a gigantic glass cabinet of sparkling silver lined with trophies and medals caught his eye.

'Look at all the awards!' Milo exclaimed.

The walls were like giant screens, and they flashed with videos and images of the school's achievements:

#2 Ranked School in the Entire World
#1 Ranked School in Ireland, four years in a row
Best for Science and Technology

These boasts were followed by the school mottos:

Efficiency in Education
Discipline Obedience Sacrifice
Unleash your potential!

'Oh, Milo,' said his mother, 'we are just so proud. Our son an Institute boy.'

'You know what this means, don't you, Milo?' said his dad and peered down over his glasses.

'Yes, Dad, it means that my future is secure,' replied Milo for the hundredth time.

'Indeed. Times are tough, Milo. You can't imagine what an advantage this opportunity is.'

All this talk of pride and opportunity had made a tiny knot in Milo's stomach. What if he messed it up? He knew the fees were astronomical.

They arrived at the convention hall with a gentle stop. It was like getting off a space shuttle.

The hall had the feel of a concert venue. Hundreds of soft red seats curved around in rows, all facing a big empty stage. Spotlights roved and pounding music blared over the babble of excited conversation. Their smart-straps pointed them to their seats.

As they sat, they had the strangest sensation: the seats moved, like massage chairs, wrapping around their bodies.

'Amazing! These must be smart-seats made by StifleCorp,' Milo's dad said.

Milo kept looking around for his two best friends, Katie and Sarah-Louise, who had also been accepted to the Institute.

Finally he spotted them, sitting several rows behind him. They didn't see him. So he stood up on his smart-seat and waved his arms like a clown to get their attention.

But before he opened his mouth to holler their names, the seat vibrated, and his biometric smart-strap buzzed, giving him a small shock. Then, without warning, a prefect was right beside him. He grabbed Milo's arm and yanked him down with brute force.

'No standing on seats,' he said in a monotone voice. His eyes were black. Milo couldn't tell whether they were angry or just empty.

He was mortified. He turned to his parents, who were shaking their heads in embarrassment and disapproval. He rubbed his arm where the prefect had grabbed him. It hurt.

Then the lights dimmed, the music changed and smoke filled the stage. Milo settled back into his seat, still rubbing his arm.

A hush descended. 'Please welcome the mastermind behind the Secondary Training Institute for Lifelong Employment, Ireland's greatest ever educator, Dr Finnegus Pummelcrush!'

A huge round of applause filled the room as Dr Pummelcrush strode across the stage. He was a big deal in Ireland. He was part saint, part intellectual, part celebrity. The people adored him for his charisma and his laser-sharp mind. The tall, thin, balding man with a slight stoop had a distinctive bounce to his walk, displaying an impressive sprightliness. He wore a flawless navy pinstriped suit.

When he reached centre stage, he smiled and raised his large bony hands, encouraging the crowd to quieten down.

'Good morning and welcome,' he bellowed in a deep, rich voice, full of charm.

Milo's parents stared at the stage in awe.

'I'd like to say to the parents and guardians: Congratulations to you! *You* have done it! Your children will flourish in life, thanks to the best education money can buy.'

The parents broke into applause and cheers.

Milo smiled at seeing his parents so happy. But a thought crossed his mind: *Why is Pummelcrush congratulating parents? It's not like* they *studied for the entrance exams.*

With the audience in the palm of his hand, Pummelcrush continued: 'Today, you join an elite and exclusive club – a club made up of winners, and winners only! Sure, we do things differently, but that is what makes us the pinnacle of excellence and success!'

He began to pace the stage. 'Never before has Ireland had a globally ranked secondary school,' he said. 'We now sit at number two in the world. Thousands of schools across the globe. And we are number two. And do you think we are happy with this?' He raised a hand to his ear.

The crowd responded with shouts of 'No!'

'That's right. We will not be satisfied until we are number one. And if my plan succeeds,' he continued, tapping the side of his head, 'by this time next year we will be the number one school in the world!'

The music exploded and a visual display of life at the Institute flashed up on the huge screen behind the stage. The atmosphere was intoxicating. Milo, sensing he was part of something historic, forgot his doubts.

Meanwhile, the prefects marched onto the stage with military precision. They each took turns in stepping forward to speak.

'The Institute has a ninety-six per cent success rate in the senior state exams.'

'At the Institute, we have reduced all forms of waste to less than three per cent.'

'The Institute will be the greatest school ever created by the end of the year.'

Each pronouncement was accompanied by cheers from the audience, who were driven to the edge of frenzy.

'Please acknowledge our prefects or, as I call them, my Disciplods,' Pummelcrush continued. 'These fine students will be representing Ireland in the exams later this year. If we want to become the number one school – it is down to these star students. Give it up for the Disciplods!'

The crowd roared as if sending warriors into battle. The prefects bowed in unison and marched off the stage.

Milo saw the admiration these students received from the crowd. He wanted people to cheer for him like that some day.

'Our curriculum focuses on the subjects that are useful in the real world.' Pummelcrush spoke with an increased sense of urgency. 'And all this is made possible by our ground-breaking Digitally Unique Personalised Education Database. Du-Ped for short. It's a super-smart technological device with twenty-four-seven real-time feedback analysis. Every minute is carefully monitored and measured by Du-Ped to ensure students get what they need for success.'

The audience lapped up every fancy buzzword.

'I must warn you now, my dear parents and guardians …'
And with this he slowed his pace, his tone changed, becoming
earnest and sincere. 'Success does not come easy. And we ask
you to place your trust in us completely. Trust us. Trust *me*.'

'We trust you!' came a random shout from the crowd,
leading to waves of laughter and yells of 'Hear, hear!'

'You might get the odd complaint from your kids about
how "strict" or "tough" we are,' he continued, making
air-quotes with his fingers. 'You might be tempted to feel
sorry for them. But stay strong! Our numbers don't lie:
ninety-six per cent graduation rate in the last ten years and
all our students get jobs. Your children will eventually adapt.
But only by committing FULLY to our system.'

Milo's parents gave him warning looks. He rolled his
eyes. It wasn't that he complained. He just liked to know
why he should do the things he was told to do. Was that
too much to ask?

'Now, I would ask you proud parents to bid your young
scholars farewell. Please make your way to the school
hyper-shop, where you will each receive a free welcome
pack, courtesy of our friends at StifleCorp. The packs come
with the latest Du-Ped operating system, so you will have
updates on your child's behaviour, health and grades.'

A final cheer and applause erupted. Pummelcrush smiled
a saintly smile, as a strange-looking woman with a clipboard
whispered in his ear.

Milo's dad shook his hand. 'Milo, we are counting on you.
Do your best at all times and you'll be fine. OK?' His dad's
voice was tense with emotion.

His mam gave him a big loving hug.

'And kids,' said Pummelcrush, 'don't worry, we haven't forgotten you. Du-Ped starter packs and some other goodies are right under your chairs.'

As the parents left, the kids were ripping open their fancy packages: smooth white boxes with the StifleCorp and Institute logos on the front. A brand-new smart-watch, a touch-screen tablet, a virtual-reality headset, Institute-branded T-shirts, runners, hats and mugs.

Milo removed the temporary smart-strap and tried on his Du-Ped watch. It automatically clasped to his small wrist and synched with his uniform. His school crest flashed yellow and the watch beeped. 'Moloney, Milo, student number 8728473' flashed up, followed by a series of graphs and tables.

Milo smiled as he looked at his new watch. He was truly part of the system now.

Chapter 2

All the sacred rights of humanity are violated
by insisting on blind obedience.
— Mary Wollstonecraft

Milo heard his name being called from a few rows back. It was Katie. He ran over to her.

Katie had long curly hair, a smile that made you think she was always in on some joke and a breezy, laid-back manner. She got up from her seat and gave her friend a hug. 'I see they actually let you in in the end?'

'I was about to ask you the same thing. Was the zoo not accepting new arrivals?' said Milo.

'Very funny.' Katie laughed and did a gentle twirl on the spot, just for fun.

Katie and Milo were neighbours and had been best friends for years.

'Sarah-Louise!' Milo shouted, disturbing her intense examination of her Du-Ped watch.

'Oh, hi, Milo!' Sarah-Louise said quietly, looking up through her thick-framed glasses and tightening her pony-tail. 'It's very good to see you. The technology here is off the charts!'

'I know. These watches are so cool. What are you doing with yours?' asked Milo.

'I'm just updating it with my information so it can give more accurate reports. You know it can record audio and video too?'

'Doing work already. Sounds about right,' said Milo, shaking his head. 'How was your summer? I haven't seen you in a while.'

'Oh, it was good. I just read a lot really, trying to prepare.'

Milo and Katie exchanged glances.

'What?' said Sarah-Louise defensively. 'It's going to be an intense year.'

The friends were just beginning to recount summer stories – disastrous camping trips, Spanish exchange students, Irish college, the time Milo fell out of a tree – when the lights dimmed again causing them to look up.

The spotlight shone on Dr Pummelcrush. But, whether it was the lighting or something else, he seemed different. In fact, the whole room seemed different. Like the shadows became more visible than the light. Pummelcrush's dense silhouette loomed large on the wall behind the stage, a sinister black figure towering over the crowd of students.

Pummelcrush stood still and surveyed the room. It felt as if a cold breeze whipped through the hall. That electrifying atmosphere of just moments ago had vanished.

'Everyone get back to your seats,' he said calmly. But his voice had changed. That warm tone had gone. It was curt and serious.

The students, many of whom had moved to talk to friends, made their way back to their seats.

Milo's smile had yet to fade, but his eyebrows furrowed.

'Now we are alone, I want you *children* to listen carefully,' said Pummelcrush, his voice quiet and steady. 'I am only going to explain this one time. And it is essential that you understand. Your entire future at this school – and your life beyond – depends on it.'

Milo noticed that the Disciplods had multiplied and taken up defensive positions along the sides of the hall. They stood with their arms behind their backs and their blank faces staring out across the auditorium.

Pummelcrush gazed out towards the students with a controlled disdain. He stood erect, frequently lifting his wart-covered hand to slick back the remaining hair on his spotted scalp.

Milo had that unsettled feeling in his stomach again. He looked around, trying to catch Katie's eye, but she was looking off into space, day-dreaming as usual. Sarah-Louise was staring at the stage, taking notes.

Pummelcrush went on in a restrained but ominous voice: 'From this moment on, you must cease to see yourself as an individual, as something separate from the Institute. It is not good enough simply to show up, attend classes and pass exams. We require a far deeper commitment.'

Milo didn't know what to think. He kept waiting for a punchline, but none came.

'Think of the school as one big organism. You are now part of the organism. You are the blood that flows through its veins. And you will flow smoothly through your time here, if – and only if – you accept your fate and surrender.'

At this the Disciplods stamped their right feet on the ground creating a massive bang that shook the audience to its core. At almost precisely the same time, the seats moved and pushed forward, forcing the students to sit bolt upright.

'Only in this way can you hope to succeed in this school. And only by succeeding in this school can you hope to survive in the real world. You must surrender yourself to the system.'

The Disciplods shouted, 'Surrender!' Then stamped their feet on the ground again.

Milo felt intimidated. He turned to his friends. He could see that, like many others, they were bewildered and frightened.

'If you do not do this, then I promise you the real world will eat you alive. You have been delivered into my care because I know how to transform messy, disobedient brats into well-behaved units capable of fitting into society.'

Pummelcrush continued, his tone even more menacing: 'For those of you too stupid to grasp what I'm saying, I will translate into language you might understand. Just do what you are told. Don't question me, don't question the system. Don't ask *any* questions at all, ever. It's that simple.'

Milo could see the other students' once bright and hopeful eyes cloud over with concern. He spotted Gerry and Liam Burke, twins from his primary school. They were strong and athletic, known for their fearlessness on the football field. But they seemed to have shrunk into their smart-seats.

Pummelcrush clenched his fists and closed his eyes, like a preacher. 'Do not think of surrender as a weakness, no. It is freedom: freedom from ever having to decide anything for yourself. Give yourselves to the system, and the rewards will be there.' He smiled the creepiest smile Milo had ever seen. 'Think of your parents and guardians. The sacrifices they have made. You have an opportunity to become part of something truly historic. Don't waste it.' He stared his cold hard stare and slowly stretched his maniacal smile wide from ear to ear. 'Now,' he said, the smile dropping immediately, 'leave.'

The Disciplods wasted no time driving the students out of the hall. The Du-Ped watches buzzed; the seats relaxed. It really was like the school was one living organism and all its parts were connected through the same consciousness.

The watches told them that class was about to begin.

Milo found Katie and Sarah-Louise as they left the hall, bundling their gifts into their Institute back-packs

'What the hell was that all about?' asked Milo, as they stood on the travellator.

'Sssh, Milo, keep your voice down,' Sarah-Louise whispered, looking all around. 'Did you see Julia Conlon got in too?'

'Yes, I saw her,' said Katie. 'Not surprising. She is pretty smart. But that was freaky, don't you think?'

'Very freaky!' Milo said a little too loudly.

'Sssh,' said Sarah-Louise again.

'Sarah-Louise, stop shushhhing me! I'll be quiet if you tell me what's an Information Transfer Centre?' Milo asked, looking at his watch

'It's what they call classrooms here,' replied Sarah-Louise, raising her voice above a whisper.

'And don't worry,' Milo went on, 'I'm sure you'll beat Julia Conlon in the class rankings.'

'Who said anything about rankings?' said Sarah-Louise.

'I really did not like that guy's energy,' said Katie. 'So creepy.'

'Yeah, I know,' said Milo. 'It's like he has a split personality.'

'Hmm,' said Sarah-Louise. 'Maybe he is just using scare tactics. Can't deny the success of the school.'

'Yeah, maybe,' said Milo.

They arrived outside their Information Transfer Centre.

'Oh dear – guess who our teacher is!' said Katie.

'Uh-oh,' said Milo.

Pummelcrush stood at the head of the room, his face somewhere between a grimace and an evil smile. 'Take your seats. No time to waste.'

The classroom, like the rest of the school, was immaculately clean. Every inch was covered in smooth white surfaces, save for the screens and sockets. It was like the entire place was made as one piece.

The Du-Ped watches directed each student to their seat.

Milo took his place at the centre of the room. As he sat, he felt the seat clench and close tight around him. The seats in the convention hall adjusted for comfort, but these seemed to trap him. He could hardly move.

The back of the seat corrected his posture. And a hard clamp tightly gripped the back of his head.

As Pummelcrush strode across the room, their heads were forced to track his movements. It was uncomfortable and weird.

'You may be surprised that I, the esteemed principal, would bother teaching first-year runts like you,' Pummelcrush snapped. 'Let's just say I have a talent for breaking in new students. It gives me a distinct pleasure to see undisciplined units become productive.'

'Did he just call us "units"?' whispered Milo to Katie, who was sitting one seat away from him.

Almost immediately, Milo felt the head-clamp pinch him. He inhaled sharply.

'You OK?' asked a skinny red-haired boy sitting between Milo and Katie. But then he inhaled quickly also.

'Did you feel that too?' Milo asked.

The boy nodded. Milo saw his name on his desk: Paul Patrick Prendergast.

He also could have sworn that Pummelcrush glanced directly at him as he whispered, even though it was impossible for him to hear.

Milo noticed the girl sitting in front of him trying to turn around, but the clamp made it impossible. He could just about see her name was Consuela Petherbridge.

'This is a state-of-the-art Information Transfer Centre. The seats, your uniforms, your watches, the cameras – all monitor and measure your heart rate, body and eye movement, breathing rate, and feed it into Du-Ped. Should your attention slip or you disrupt my session, either I or the system will punish you immediately.' As he said this last line, he pulled a long steel baton from the side of his podium.

'Your job is simple: keep your mouth shut, don't ask questions and pay attention at all times.'

He smacked the baton down. As it hit the desk, a jolt of electricity buzzed at the end of it.

Sarah-Louise, seated in front of Milo, gasped.

'I said mouths shut,' Pummelcrush said coolly.

A fearful atmosphere fell across the class.

Then Milo shot up his hand. Before Pummelcrush had a chance to react, Milo blurted out, 'But, sir, what if I have to go to the toilet and the seat traps me in? Actually, I think I have to go now, sir. Can I go to the toilet? Please, sir?'

For the first time, Pummelcrush looked surprised. He raised one of his thick hairy eyebrows.

Milo yelped in pain as he received a sharp pinch to the back of his neck from a pair of rubber fingers. 'Ow, my neck!'

Pummelcrush smiled, curling his lip upward. 'Toilet breaks and everything else are governed by Du-Ped. It knows when you have to go. But open your mouth in my class again, boy, and it's more than a toilet break you will need.'

Milo, rubbing the back of his neck, whispered to Katie, 'How is Du-Ped supposed to know when I have to go to the toilet? *I* don't even know when I have to go half the time.'

'What? You mean you go sometimes without realising?' Katie whispered, trying to stifle a giggle.

'Hey, it's a crazy world, a lot of stuff happens.'

Paul Patrick couldn't help but laugh along, his shoulders bouncing as he did so.

Just then all three of them jumped in their seats, letting out small cries of agony.

This time, a short, sharp electro-shock had been delivered through their smart-seats directly onto their right butt cheeks.

It felt to Milo like someone had poked him with a red-hot needle. It stung like hell.

'Ouch, my butt!' Milo screamed, sending the class into fits of nervous laughter, which led to more pinches and butt shocks, until the whole class was yelping and laughing in equal measure.

'What is going on in this place?' Paul Patrick screamed.

Some students, including Consuela, gasped, and tears filled their eyes as it seemed like all hell broke loose.

'QUIET!' shouted Pummelcrush. 'Well,' he said, 'in all my years, I have never encountered such a brazen group of misfits. But that's fine,' he said, regaining his composure, 'if that's how you want it. All the more satisfying for me to watch you all get put in your place. Now, recite with me the daily incantation.'

Pummelcrush closed his eyes and spoke the school poem, while the class joined in:

> *I aspire to surrender my mind, my body and my soul.*
> *I surrender them to the almighty, all-knowing system.*
> *For it is through surrender that we learn discipline*
> *And it is through discipline that we reach success.*

The students had been instructed to learn this off before arriving. Milo was still angry and in real pain. As a protest, he thought he would not say the incantation. But as he looked up and met Pummelcrush's eyes, he felt the clamp tighten.

He joined in.

'Let us begin,' said Pummelcrush. He launched into the lesson plan. It began with maths. Equations and theorems were thrown out one after the other for forty minutes. Then he moved on to biology, economics and physics.

At the Institute, each class had just one teacher for the year. They boasted that teachers were almost obsolete. The Du-Ped system dictated everything. The teacher was merely a delivery channel. All the other teachers were loyal past pupils.

Du-Ped monitored the students' focus and note-taking, and constantly updated their personalised study plans for their weekly tests.

There was no room for excuses. Milo and his class had no choice but to follow at the blistering pace of the lesson. The discomfort of the smart-seats, tight around their thighs and pushing into their lower back, along with the moving head-clamps, made any relaxation impossible.

Each forty-minute segment was so jam-packed with information that it would fly by, but was mentally exhausting.

Lunch break came around quickly, and the students were finally released. Most took the opportunity to stretch their necks and backs. But they were immediately forced to jump on the travellator to be brought to the canteen.

The canteen was huge. It contained lots of round white tables. The travellators took the students around the room to collect bowls, cutlery and food from a series of massive dispensers. A grey sludge squelched out of the dispenser in a single plop. Nutri-paste, they called it. They were told it was a nutritious paste made from the produce of the school's vegetable garden, expertly designed to provide all the necessary vitamins, amino acids, omega oils and minerals young humans needed to grow, stay healthy and keep focused. They were then delivered to their pre-assigned seats. They were like a stream of ants moving in perfect harmony, except they were carrying trays with bowls of stodgy grey food that actual ants wouldn't eat.

The sludge not only looked like rotten garbage, it tasted like it too. Even Sarah-Louise admitted it was difficult to eat, although she was adamant that it was good for you.

After lunch, they had thirty minutes to exercise in the purpose-built yard. Signs everywhere said:

> No playing allowed
> No games
> Serious exercise only

The exercise they were allowed was alternating between a brisk walk and sprinting at short intervals. This was enough to get the heart pumping, which helped concentration.

'What's the story with this place?' asked Milo in between sprints. 'Is this some kind of joke? I keep waiting for everyone to say, "Gotcha" and then for normal school to start.'

'Guys, stop complaining!' said Sarah-Louise. 'I'm sure it's just a way to get us to concentrate and settle in fast.'

'I dunno,' said Katie. 'I feel ill from lunch, and my backside still hurts.'

'Same,' agreed Milo. 'What if our butts fall off from too many shocks?'

They laughed, but Sarah-Louise looked around uneasily. 'Was it really sore?'

'Yes!' answered Katie.

'Oh, I'm sorry.' Sarah-Louise put out her arms to give her friends a double-hug. 'We will have to be extra careful to stay out of trouble.'

Milo wondered whether he could do that. The thought of this brutal routine every day made his throat tighten.

When the thirty minutes were up, the travellator zoomed them back to class.

Business studies, computer science and accounting took them through the rest of the afternoon. There were no more outbursts or shocks that day. But at one point a blaring siren went off in order to wake people up. Several times Milo's mind wandered, until his focus was jolted back into place by the head-clamp.

Finally, the lessons ended with a loud buzzer. The seats relaxed, watches beeped and head-clamps retracted. It was like the whole room let out a sigh of relief.

'Lessons are over, but the day is not. You have time allotted after supper to review and memorise everything we covered today. It will be tested at the end of the week,' Pummelcrush said matter-of-factly. 'Whoever is last in the quiz will be punished.'

One day into their new lives and the students of class 1FP (1 Finnegus Pummelcrush) were exhausted.

They trudged out in a stupefied daze.

They made their way through the shiny bright corridors to the dormitories in silence. The only time Milo looked up from the ground was when a few students were bulldozed by a group of Disciplods making their way down the hall. It was like they didn't even see other people.

He reached his bed, one rectangle among many identical stations. There was a small locker with an automated lamp that could not be turned on or off. In fact, Milo noticed that about just about everything in the school: lights, toilets, doors, even the ground itself. There were no switches or buttons. There was nothing that allowed you to exert any control on the school or have any power over anything. Everything was centrally administered and pre-programmed to be used as efficiently as possible.

At first he'd found it fascinating. The travellators and the seats. But now it seemed frustrating and disturbing. Milo felt like an object, a robot.

He changed into the burgundy school tracksuit. He sat for a moment and contemplated having a short nap. But just as he began to close his heavy eyes, a sharp wrist buzz ordered him to the canteen for supper.

The ants marched and inhaled another bowl of sludgy, bland nutri-paste.

Then it was straight to the study hall. It was deathly silent for a massive room full of eight hundred teenagers. They recited the school incantation again; all the older students shouting it with the crazed intensity of football fans.

Several pairs of Disciplods patrolled the hall, administering shocks through their watches to anyone who dared to daydream or talk. Study ended at nine o'clock. There was thirty minutes to get ready for bed.

Milo lay for a moment wondering if this was really the price of success. Who would he become after six years? Would he turn out like the Disciplods?

But then, he thought of his parents, the school's reputation. How everyone praised it. Could they all be wrong? *Surely not,* he thought. *Maybe I'll get used to it after a while.*

But deep down inside him an alarm was going off. *Can anything be worth this?* he thought.

Chapter 3

All cruelty springs from weakness.
     – Seneca

The next morning, Milo's alarm went off at four-thirty. Milo assumed that was a mistake, clicked his watch and rolled over, returning to a cosy sleep.

Three minutes later, the alarm went off again. Half asleep, he clicked the watch once more. *There's no way it's time to get up,* he thought. He began to hear other students stirring. Then: SLAM! The smart-bed shot up on one side and he slid off like a sack of spuds and landed on the ground with a thud.

It turned out that class started at half-past five in the morning!

Still in shock, Milo found Katie and Sarah-Louise at breakfast. Gerry and Liam were sitting with Paul Patrick at the next table. They nodded; everyone was too tired to talk. Well, almost everyone.

'Ready for another day?' asked Sarah-Louise, full of energy.

'Ah would you stop', muttered Gerry.

'Not so loud, jeez,' answered Katie. She yawned and stretched.

'Yippee,' Milo said sarcastically, raising his two thumbs limply. 'I can't wait. Woo. Hoo.'

Back in class, Dr Pummelcrush didn't waste a second. From five-thirty on the dot, he ploughed through the lesson plans and shovelled information into their young minds.

The day played out like a mirror image of the previous one, not a moment to catch a breath.

And so did the next day.

And the next.

The passage of time began to feel strange and unfamiliar: days would seem infinitely long, but weeks would fly by in the blink of an eye. Day in, day out, the exact same thing: wake up, sludge, class, sludge, exercise, class, sludge, study, bed. It felt like there was no today or tomorrow, just one nightmarish present moment. Before they could blink, they had been at the school for a month.

The only evidence of a changing outside world were the brief glimpses they would catch of important visitors meeting with Pummelcrush, or the construction work going on for a new east wing of the school. Any communication with family or friends was brief and superficial. There was a rumour that Du-Ped monitored all texts and communication with the outside world so that the school could track the students' true feelings and catch any potential complainers. It felt to Milo like being in a zoo. From the outside looking in, a zoo seems like a fun place. But for animals looking out, it might be a monotonous prison.

The gruelling schedule was beginning to take its toll on the new students. He and his friends were barely there a month and they were exhausted. Dark circles had taken shape under everyone's bloodshot eyes. Some students developed nervous twitches. Nail-biting became a popular pastime.

In particular, Sarah-Louise was really struggling. One morning in mid-October Milo noticed that she wasn't looking her usual cheery self. In fact, he thought she looked awful.

'Are you feeling OK, Sarah-Louise?' he asked.

'Yes, I'm fine, of course,' she snapped.

He looked at her as they made their way to class. Her eyes were like a raccoon's – with big dark rings around them. The skin around her nose was raw and red; tiny beads of sweat glistened across her forehead.

'You don't look fine,' said Milo.

'Thanks a bunch, Milo,' said Sarah-Louise and darted off ahead of him.

'Wait, that's not what I meant. I mean, you always look good. It's just you don't look *well*. You get me?'

'Yes, I get it. I'm just a little run-down, that's all. But I'm fine,' she replied through sniffles and a cough. 'The schedule here is somewhat tough, especially if you want to get a good ranking.'

Milo knew that Sarah-Louise was locked in a battle with Julia Conlon for the number one spot. It seemed to be getting the better of her.

'You are a legend! You're top of the class almost every week,' said Milo, trying to make up for his blunder. 'But maybe take it a bit easy and rest up this weekend?'

They arrived at class. They had learned to stop talking just as they approached the classroom. Too many times already, conversations had accidentally run on into the room and once they were seated the students would get a retro-active pinch or shock.

When they sat down, Sarah-Louise was looking even worse than before. It was like the clamp was the only thing holding her head up.

About half an hour into class, while a huge display of the chemical make-up of salt appeared on the smart-wall, Milo heard Sarah-Louise groan. The groan was quickly followed by a yelp of pain. Everyone knew what that meant. A butt shock for making a noise out of turn. Her first one.

Pummelcrush let the system take care of these minor infractions and didn't even look up: 'The chemical make-up of salt is NaCl.' But he stopped mid-sentence and looked up when he heard another groan and a yelp. He rolled his eyes and removed his glasses.

'I thought I was finished with this nonsense. Don't you know how things work by now, you complete idiot?' He stared at Sarah-Louise.

'I'm sorry, sir, it's just that I really don't feel well. May I be excused to see the nurse?' Sarah-Louise spoke politely with barely a whimper. Milo knew that it must be serious for Sarah-Louise to make such a request, to potentially sacrifice her number one position.

Pummelcrush checked his screen. 'No,' he snapped. 'Sodium chloride, commonly known as salt, is an ionic compound –'

'Please, sir, I don't feel good. I need to lie down. *Ouch!*' screamed Sarah-Louise, as the pincher, a small pair of rubber fingers, reached out from the head-clamp and squeezed a piece of skin on her neck. It was excruciating: much worse than the shock in fact, as Milo had found out numerous times.

'I can't believe I have to say this again,' Pummelcrush said, doing his best to remain calm. 'If you were sick, Du-Ped would have informed us. Therefore, you are a faking, lying brat.'

Milo could feel the whole room seize up. It was blatantly obvious Sarah-Louise wasn't well. You didn't need a computer to tell you that. Surely Pummelcrush knew that Sarah-Louise – of all people – wouldn't lie.

But none of them, Milo included, could open their mouths. They had to swallow the frustration.

Pummelcrush went back to the lesson, but was quickly interrupted once more by Sarah-Louise.

'I'm not faking, sir. Please! I feel awful.'

'I said no!'

In a burst of emotion, Milo shouted: 'Just let her out. She is sick. This isn't fair! You don't need a stupid Du-Ped to tell you that! It's obvious. How do you expect us to respect you if you're not fair!?'

Du-Ped's revenge was instant and brutal, immediately issuing a series of pinches and shocks to Milo's neck, back and butt.

Realising what he had just done, Milo looked around and saw pure fear in Paul Patrick Prendergast's eyes.

Gasps of disbelief spread across the room.

Pummelcrush stepped out from behind his podium and moved toward Sarah-Louise like a panther circling his prey.

'You will feel sick when we tell you to feel sick.' He squeezed the words out of his mouth, twisted with disgust and anger, but trying to appear poised. 'Now, for the last time, shut up and pay attention.'

And then he pointed his electrified baton at Milo and turned his head slowly to face him, still standing right in front of Sarah-Louise.

'And you ...' he said, staring at Milo, 'did you just dare to speak out of turn in my classroom? Did you just dare to question me?' He remained composed, but he looked ready to explode.

Milo was panicked. 'Yes, sir – I'm sorry, sir. I just, thought ... I mean I think ... that if someone ...'

'Shut your stupid brazen mouth,' Pummelcrush snapped, his electric baton ablaze with cracks and sizzles, his eyes burning with hatred.

Milo was terrified. He felt in real physical danger. He thought he heard Katie crying. This was bad, really bad. He wanted to grab both his friends and run away. But he was trapped; they all were.

'In all my thirty-five years of teaching, I haven't met any student as downright stupid as you, Moloney. What is wrong with you?' Pummelcrush's tone rose with each word. 'You think you can waltz into the greatest school that ever existed, and tell me what to do? You make me sick.'

And just as he said the word 'sick', Sarah-Louise opened her mouth and spewed forth a gushing stream of vomit onto

Pummelcrush's clean navy wool suit. Watery yellow-grey slime was pouring out of her mouth, bursting forth like a fireman's hose. And all of it – every last drop – found its way onto Pummelcrush, who stood paralysed in horror as he watched his crisp trousers turn soggy with human barf. Flecks of Sarah-Louise's spew splashed their way up his shirt and onto his red tie.

And then, she stopped. It was like someone turned off the pipe at the source. And Sarah-Louise, her head bowed and limp from the physical toll of vomiting, a drip of excess saliva falling from her lip, slowly looked up at Pummelcrush as she wiped her mouth with her sleeve.

The class sat in suspended animation.

Pummelcrush stood there, frozen to the spot, as if the puke had rendered him immobile. His expression was of pure shock and revulsion. Everyone knew how much he cared about cleanliness and hygiene. The seconds ticked by and the class waited for what would happen next.

Milo, giddy with excitement, couldn't hold it in any longer: 'Excuse me, Dr Pummelpuke, I mean, Pukelcrush, there's a bit of sick just there on your suit.'

The tension broke and giggles bubbled up all over the class.

Pummelcrush lost it completely.

'SHUT YOUR MOUTH, MOLONEY!' he shouted. He pointed the baton at Milo and clicked a button that gave him a full-body shock. Milo screamed in pain. Pummelcrush pulled out his handkerchief and began cleaning himself.

The class immediately quietened down.

'You did that on purpose, didn't you?' he shouted at Sarah-Louise, his face twisted with rage. 'You made yourself sick deliberately. You disgusting little rat. You will sit here for the rest of the day. We will get through this lesson plan if it takes me all day and all night!'

He turned to Milo: 'You, GET OUT OF MY CLASS-ROOM! You're a pathetic disgrace.'

As he yelled, flecks of white and yellow spit flew from his mouth. The unfortunate students seated in the front row looked like they had just ridden a rollercoaster, their hands slapped flat on the desks and their eyes wide open.

'The Disciplods will deal with you!'

Milo's seat relaxed. He rose, trembling with fear. He was afraid of Pummelcrush, there was no doubt, but the Disciplods really creeped him out.

Katie went to grab his hand as he walked past. He could see in her eyes she was about to speak up on his behalf. But Milo quickly shot her a look that said, *Don't you dare. It's bad enough* I'm *in this mess.*

Chapter 4

Wonder is the feeling of a philosopher,
and philosophy begins in wonder.
— Plato

The door shut and Milo stood alone in a pristine white corridor. There wasn't a soul to be seen.

He doubled over, still feeling the pain of the full body shock. Now *he* felt sick. Sick and lonely: that strange kind of loneliness when you are not only by yourself, but you're supposed to be somewhere else, with everyone else.

Milo was no stranger to getting in trouble. But never did he fear for his life. And then came the self-loathing: *Why can't you just keep your stupid mouth shut?* he repeated to himself.

And then another sickening thought: his parents were probably going to find out. They probably already had.

He heard footsteps coming. They had the urgent, rhythmic precision of the Disciplods. *Clip-clop, clip-clop.*

Milo panicked. Would they beat him up? Or shock him? He spotted two big Disciplods turning the corner, about ten metres away. They were walking right towards him, with that same unsettling dead-eyed stare.

*Screw thi*s, and without thinking, he bolted in the opposite direction.

He got to the end of the corridor and reached one of the glass tunnels connecting part of the school to the centre of the complex.

He heard the Disciplods shouting: 'Stop now, student 8728473. You are not allowed to run indoors. Disobedience will not be tolerated.'

Bloody hell, thought Milo, *even their threats are boring.*

He turned the corner and kept running, careful to keep his balance on the slick floor. He could hear their footsteps speed up. Before he knew it, they were turning the corner behind him.

Milo halted momentarily when he saw another two Disciplods emerging onto the fourth floor from the stairwell in front of him. He was trapped.

He ran directly at the two new Disciplods. He knew they were slow, and he was fast. He knew they were big, and he was small. And he also knew the ground was so shiny that it would be perfect for sliding.

As he approached, they widened their stance to block the corridor and grab him. But Milo gracefully transformed his sprint into a slide and ducked right between the legs of the Disciplod on the left. As he slid, he saw them looking down between their legs, just as the other two arrived.

He saw one of them – the same one who'd yanked him off the chair at orientation – clicking a button and pointing his watch at him.

Milo had just got back on his feet to keep running towards the travellator when – BAM! – his whole body froze. He felt half-paralysed.

What's going on? he thought. *Have they shot a poison dart at me? Was it a taser?*

Then he realised that his body was fine, it was his uniform. It had become stiff like cardboard. They must be able to control the uniforms with their watches.

Sprinting became immensely difficult, but he could still move. He was just a few metres away from the hand-rail of the travellator that led to the ground floor.

He summoned all his strength and focused it into a few more steps. Just as the Disciplods arrived to grab him, he burst forward and leapt over the railing and grabbed the side of the travellator.

'Go after him,' said one of the Disciplods.

'Jumping over the barrier is against the rules.'

'Our orders are to catch him,' said another.

'Hanging off the side of the travellator is against the rules.'

While they argued about which rule was most important, Milo hung on tight to the railing as he was taken down through the floors of the Institute. As he got further away, he felt his uniform soften and return to normal.

It must only work within certain distances, he thought.

He reached the ground floor and darted off down another corridor towards the part of the school where the vegetable gardens were. He opened the first door he saw and ducked inside.

His heart was beating fast and sweat was dripping off his face as he shut the door behind him. He heard the Disciplods marching past.

Milo exhaled a sigh of relief and then started to giggle. Here he was, crouched in some random dark closet in the most prestigious school in Ireland, after being kicked out of class and dodging the Disciplods. *Funny how I can still laugh, even when things are bad.*

His senses slowly adjusted to the darkness. He could have sworn he heard music. He realised that apart from the orientation ceremony, he hadn't heard a single note of music since coming here. Milo loved music. He dreamed of being a musician one day. But it wasn't taught here. It was 'a waste', not useful for the 'real world'.

He followed the sound and moved deeper into the black space. He found another door handle at the back of the closet. He turned it and pulled the door open, and the music poured into his ears.

He smiled. What he saw before him was a bright and beautiful little garden. It was surrounded by the school's white walls, which were mostly hidden by green climbing plants. Every part of the garden was bursting with splashes of colour from flowerpots and hanging baskets: strong bright reds; brilliant dancing yellows; deep dense purples.

Milo inhaled deeply. He recognised the scent of lavender.

All along one wall were shelves full of old books and half-finished paintings, covered by a canvas awning. There were a few old musical instruments, a trumpet and a ukulele, beside all sorts of strange globes and ornaments from different cultures: an African mask, a Japanese scroll, a small statue that looked South American.

There was a beautiful tree in the middle of the garden. It was magnificent and old; its trunk thick and strong.

He stepped forward to touch it, but just then he saw someone in the corner of the garden. He jumped back in fright. *Not more trouble*, he thought. There, bent over some flowerpots, pouring water from a green watering can, was a small, elegant old woman. She clearly hadn't heard him come in. She was busy humming to the music. He considered running away, but something about the garden made him feel at ease.

'Excuse me,' he croaked, his voice shaky after his escape.

The small woman let out a gasp and turned with a fright, dropping the watering can.

'I'm sorry!' Milo said quickly to put her at ease. 'I didn't mean to sneak up on you.'

'Good grief, young man,' she said as she laid her green-gloved hand across her chest. 'What are you doing here? Shouldn't you be in class?'

She had short silver hair, sallow skin and big kind brown eyes.

'Yes, Miss, I'm supposed to be. But ...' he sputtered, half-considering making up a lie. He sighed. 'But I got kicked out. And then ... well ... I ran off because those creepy Disciplods were chasing me. I came in here to hide.' Milo was unsure why he was being so honest.

'I see.' She smiled at him and he instantly relaxed. 'And what, pray tell, did you get kicked out for?'

'That's the thing!' he exclaimed. 'It's that bloody Dr Pummelcrush. He was being so mean to my friend Sarah-Louise. You see, she was sick – like, properly ill. It was obvious, and he wouldn't let her out to see the nurse. Soooo ... I said some stuff and got kicked out.'

'What stuff?' she asked, peering at him.

'Hmm, I can't really remember,' replied Milo, avoiding her eyes. 'Something about how his Du-Ped system is stupid, and he is treating us unfairly, and maybe we would respect him if he was fair.'

'You said all that to Dr Pummelcrush?' she asked, her face breaking into a grin. 'Wow! What's your name?'

Milo wasn't sure if she was impressed or shocked.

'Milo Moloney. What's yours?'

'I'm Ursula Joy. It's a pleasure to meet you.' They shook hands.

Milo sat down on a small bench beside the tree. 'I don't know why I didn't keep my mouth shut like everyone else. I don't know what's wrong with me. I knew I'd get in trouble. Now what's going to happen to me? Probably be assassinated.'

'Now, wait just a minute, young man. There is no need for talk like that,' Ursula said in a slow, deliberate way, moving towards him. 'I think you asked some excellent and reasonable questions. I don't think there is anything wrong with you.'

'Really?' said Milo, surprised. He was used to adults telling him to be quiet and to do what he was told.

'Quite the opposite, in fact: it sounds to me like you were raising some very thoughtful philosophical questions.'

'I was? Philosophical? What's philosophical?' asked Milo. 'I mean, I knew I did that, but I just want to know what you think it is.'

Ursula laughed. 'You questioned his ideas of fairness, of authority and of knowledge. They are all important philosophical ideas.'

'They are?' Milo was intrigued that there could be a name for the kinds of questions he had asked.

'Yes, they are. I should know, I used to teach philosophy here many years ago, before all the changes.'

'You did? How come you don't any more?'

'Dr Pummelcrush banned it shortly after he took over, along with music and art. He said they weren't useful for passing exams and getting jobs, that they were a distraction. But, honestly, I think he didn't like the way philosophy made young people challenge him. He hates being challenged.'

'He banned it? Wait – what *is* philosophy?'

Ursula's eyes lit up and she took a deep breath before answering.

'That is not an easy question to answer,' she said, 'because philosophy is about everything! Well, it's about questioning everything. It's about questioning things that we think we know for sure, things that we take for granted. It's one of humanity's oldest attempts to understand ourselves and the world around us. Philosophy doesn't assume anything is true already. Everything is up for grabs, from the ultimate nature of the universe and where it came from, to how we should treat one another, to what is right and wrong. But really, it starts with simple wonder – wonder, curiosity and openness towards the absolute craziness of the situation we find ourselves in.'

Milo was immediately entranced by Ursula's passion. It made him curious. 'What do you mean, our "situation"?' he asked.

Ursula began to gently pace around the garden, gesticulating softly with her delicate hands.

'The human situation. Being a human in the world. It's so strange! Don't you think? You, me, all of us. Human existence in the universe. I mean, think about it. The very fact that we find ourselves – through absolutely no choice of our own – just one day thrown onto a planet, in a solar system, in a gigantic cosmic space called the universe. We don't know where it all came from, what it's made from, why we are here, or what we are supposed to do with our time! Life at its most basic is a mystery, yet we have no choice but to keep living it and do our best to figure out the right way to live as we muddle along. Have you ever thought about those kinds of things, Milo?'

'Yeah! I mean, I've thought sometimes about how strange everything is.'

'Strange! Bizarre! Absurd! And yet, we act like everything is normal. And what's more, we humans have this remarkable ability to use language. We can make sounds with our mouths or draw squiggles on a page and communicate all sorts of ideas, thoughts and feelings to one another. And whether it's a blessing or a curse, it allows us to ask and try to answer all these questions: Does life have a meaning? What happens after we die? Is there a god? And if so, who made god? Is the purpose of life to be happy? Successful? Rich? Is freedom more important than justice? Why is there so much suffering in the world? These are philosophical questions. And they are fascinating and fun to explore, and I just don't know why we don't talk about them more often!'

Milo sat on the bench under the shade of the great tree, staring up at Ursula as she spoke, freely following her movements, nodding along. He felt for a moment like his mind and body had expanded to the size of the cosmos, like he was a giant human floating around space looking down on the planets and the stars, and he could zoom right in to see earth and all the humans on it running around doing all the strange things they do. It was exhilarating.

Many of the questions Ursula asked were things he had thought or felt before, but never articulated or discussed with anyone. When he lay in bed looking at the stars from his bedroom window, wondering what was out there in space. Or when he watched the news and saw all the terrible things that were happening and wondered why.

Ursula kept pacing calmly. Her face was full of excitement and happiness, but she always remained firmly rooted in the moment with Milo: it made him feel like he was the only person in the world, and she was really speaking to him, not just at him, like most adults. He really felt like he existed.

'I think I understand,' said Milo. 'I suppose I figured that, at a certain point, we had to just accept that this is the way things are. You know? Like we can't question everything – but maybe we can?'

'Yes, of course we can – exactly, Milo.'

It was as if she had been waiting for an opportunity to talk about this stuff for a very long time.

'This is where philosophy comes in,' Ursula went on. 'Philosophy is our attempt to figure out what on earth is going on, and to share our sense of wonder with one another so we don't feel so alone and confused. Because if there is one thing I'm sure of, it's that everyone in the world has these thoughts at some point.'

'I never knew you could talk about these things,' said Milo. 'I always felt that these were just secret weird thoughts that you had, but you had to ignore them and get on with things in the real world.'

'Pff, the "real world". I hate that phrase. What does it even mean? What is more real than asking about the ultimate nature of reality? Or trying to figure out the best way to live a good life? Or the right way to take care of each other?'

'I guess those things are pretty important.'

'Milo, humans have been discussing these things for thousands of years – your thoughts are not weird, they are the most human of all thoughts. We have just lost the space to speak about them in public. I fear people have lost a sense of wonder at their own existence.'

'I think my head is about to explode!'

Ursula laughed. 'That is completely normal, Milo. Don't worry about understanding everything I say. Philosophy is something that you come to understand over time, by doing it. And the more you talk about and explore these questions, the less overwhelming and intimidating they become.'

'Oh, I like it, don't get me wrong! It's just a lot to take in. It's, like, philosophy asks the questions that we don't have answers to, right?'

'Yes, that's a good way of putting it. Philosophy is interested in the wondrous mystery of existence. It's interested in exploring those deep dark places that remain unknown.

Philosophy is humble. It doesn't assume that we know everything already. Philosophy is open-minded; it's OK with the possibility that things may be radically different than we think. But most of all, it helps you think for yourself. You can't look up the internet to find the answers to these questions.'

'But wait. If philosophy is about all these big questions about the universe and how we live, then how was what I said to Dr Pummelcrush philosophy?'

'Because you questioned his assumptions. And philosophy is all about questioning assumptions, questioning what we assume we know, or take for granted. Every day we assume things without realising it. We obey certain rules, treat each other in a certain way and have certain beliefs about the way things are. Usually, we just kind of accept things because everybody else does. But you challenged these beliefs. Your challenge was to ask why do we have to obey authority even when it doesn't seem fair? And you asked why he trusts the system over his own eyes? Philosophy asks how do we know when to believe something is true. These are classic philosophical questions, Milo.'

'I didn't know that was philosophy too. But I think about this all the time! At home and at school, we are always getting told rules to follow but never given reasons why. I hate it.'

'One of the main ideas in philosophy is that we should not accept something as true just because someone else says it is true, even if that person is famous or powerful. We need to discuss things together in an open conversation. And that works for children and adults.'

Milo felt he might have found something that could help him understand all his thoughts and feelings about the world and about being told what to do.

'I think I like philosophy!'

'I thought you might. I could see it in your eyes. But be careful with it too. Philosophy is not about rejecting everything you are told, disobeying every rule or arguing with everyone all the time. You must be open to listening to what others have to say. You remind me of myself, you know. I was young and curious like you, but it got me in trouble. So be cautious. It's about questioning what we are told, seeking reasons, but doing so with an open mind and heart so we can find a better way to live our short lives on earth together.'

MILO: But how do we know when it's right to obey authority and when it's better to challenge it?

URSULA: That's a good question, and here is the other thing about philosophy: there is often no simple answer. There is no perfect rule to follow to know when it's right to challenge authority. But you can develop better judgement, weigh up each situation to try and find the best approach!

MILO: What do you mean?

URSULA: Well, what made you think it was wrong of Dr Pummelcrush to treat your friend the way he did?

MILO: It just wasn't fair. And everyone knew it wasn't fair.

URSULA: But how do we know when something is fair or unfair?

MILO: It was obvious she was sick. But he didn't care. He just wanted to follow Du-Ped. To me that's not fair. If someone is sick, they need help to feel better.

URSULA: So, when someone is sick, they deserve to be treated differently from someone who is not sick?

MILO: Yes, definitely.

URSULA: Well, maybe fairness is about treating people how they deserve to be treated, depending on the situation?

MILO: Hmm, I always thought fairness was more about treating people equally. Like it's fair when everyone gets the same size slice of cake, or the same amount of time playing video games.

URSULA: Yes, I think that is true a lot of the time – when everyone deserves to be treated the same way. But that is not always the case.

MILO: But if fairness is treating people how they deserve to be treated, then how do we know what people deserve?

URSULA: Ohhh, now you're getting it. That's another big and difficult philosophical question. We make these kinds of decisions all the time: we treat our friends and family differently than strangers. We treat the elderly differently to the young. We treat children differently to adults.

MILO: I never thought of it like that. I thought we had to treat everyone the same. Isn't that equality?

URSULA: Yes, even though we treat people differently all the time, everyone deserves a basic level of respect.

That is why we have something called human rights.

MILO: I've heard of human rights.

URSULA: Great! So what are they?

MILO: Oh, I dunno. I just heard the name.

URSULA: Well, you're human. Make up your own! It's just us talking, let's see how we do. If you were making your own world, what would you want every person to have a right to?

MILO: I'd say everyone has the right to food? Is that silly?

URSULA: Not at all, for sure everyone has the right to the basic things they need to survive and live.

MILO: Cool – so food, a house or some kind of shelter, ummm, to feel safe?

URSULA: Great! So far so good I'd say. What else?

MILO: The right to do whatever you want to do with your life, maybe.

URSULA: But what if someone wants to spend their life hurting others?

MILO: Good point – so the right to do what you want without hurting anyone else.

URSULA: Freedom, within limits. Sounds about right. Go on.

MILO: Hmm, the right not to do something you don't want to. Like, someone shouldn't be able to force you to do things you don't want to do.

URSULA: Interesting. One of the main human rights is the right not to be enslaved – slavery is against human rights. But what about things like work or school, Milo?

MILO: That's what I was thinking. Is it fair to be forced to come to school? Nobody forces adults to do things.

URSULA: What about work? Aren't people forced to work jobs in order to survive?

MILO: But that's different – they could quit if they wanted.

URSULA: But then they might starve or become homeless. Are they really free to quit?

MILO: Oh, yeah, hmm. That's true. I mean, I get why school is needed, but why does it have to be so annoying?

URSULA: It doesn't, Milo. Education could be a joyful, wonderful experience.

MILO: I wish you were still teaching here, Ursula. I bet I would have liked your philosophy classes!

URSULA: Oh so do I, Milo.

Milo checked his watch. 'Oh, look at the time. How come my beeper didn't go for supper? I have to go in three minutes.'

'The Du-Ped system doesn't work in here. I made sure of that.'

'Really? How? What is this place?'

'I'm the school gardener, responsible for the vegetable garden,' said Ursula. 'After they decided to cut art, philosophy and music, I fought with Pummelcrush for months. It got nasty. Eventually he bullied me into submission, but they let me stay on as gardener as a gesture of good will to see out my retirement.'

'But there are no vegetables in here?'

'No. This is my own secret private garden, so don't tell anyone. It's connected through that tunnel to the greenhouses.' Ursula pointed to a passageway leading out of the garden.

'It's a lovely place.'

'Thank you. Everything in the main vegetable garden is grown for a purpose; to be packaged and sold for profit. I wanted somewhere quiet where I could come and grow plants I thought were beautiful just for their own sake.'

'I'm glad I stumbled into it.' Milo had never met an adult who talked to him like a real person.

'Me too,' replied Ursula.

'It just goes to show,' said Milo, 'good things happen when you get kicked out of class and escape from the Disciplods.'

They laughed.

'We shouldn't be laughing, Milo. I don't want you getting in any more trouble.'

'I'll try my best, but it won't be easy.'

'How about we make a deal? I let you come back to my garden and I can teach you little bits of philosophy. You can ask all the questions you like. That way you'll get to release your frustration without getting in trouble, and I'll get to do philosophy again after all these years! But you have to promise to keep out of trouble. How does that sound?'

'It's a deal,' said Milo, delighted at the chance to come back to this lovely little garden and hang out with Ursula. He got up to leave.

'Great! And between you and me, those Disciplods creep me out too.'

'There is something very strange about them.'

'Indeed. Sometimes I wonder about this place,' she said, staring into the distance.

'What do you mean?'

'I don't know. I've noticed some odd things over the years. Kids start out as bright-eyed, hopeful students, full of energy and curiosity – just like you. Then within a few years they are flat and lifeless: no questions, no playing, no laughing.'

'I noticed that too! It can't be good, can it?'

'I really don't know, maybe I'm just old fashioned. Well, you'd better go!'

'It was great to meet you. Hopefully I'll see you soon.'

And with that he was gone, back through the dark closet and out into the bright, shiny corridor.

Milo sprinted along the travellator at double-speed to the canteen – just in time to slot in with Katie and Sarah-Louise.

They threw their arms around him.

Sarah-Louise still looked terrible. 'Milo, are you OK?' she asked. 'I wish you had kept your mouth shut, but thanks for sticking up for me! You're a good pal.'

'Don't worry about me, Sarah-Louise,' said Milo. 'And how are *you*?' He was shocked to see her there. 'Did he not let you go to the nurse?'

'Oh, I'm fine now,' she said. 'No need to trouble the nurse.'

'He didn't let her go,' said Katie, shaking her head. 'Can you believe that? It's so mean. But what happened to you?'

'Don't tell anyone, but,' he leaned closer to whisper, 'the Disciplods were sent after me. But I gave them the Milo-slip.'

'Ha! The Milo-slip?' asked Katie. 'That's not a thing.'

'It could be, though. I ran away, slid between their legs, jumped off the balcony, coasted down the travellator, hid out – and found this secret garden.'

'You did *what*?' asked Sarah-Louise sternly.

'But then I met this kind lady, the school gardener. She was cool. I'll introduce you.'

Sarah-Louise and Katie exchanged worried glances.

'Milo, are you making this up?' asked Katie. 'This sounds made-up.'

'No, I swear!'

'You met a lady in a secret garden after escaping the Disciplods?'

'Yes, Katie.'

'Why are you smiling, Milo?' asked Sarah-Louise. 'You missed more class. Remember, we have a quiz on Friday. Pummelcrush hates you even more. The Disciplods will want revenge.'

'Well, when you put it like that, it sounds bad. But the more I find out about this place, the more I get the feeling it's worse than we think. We need to –'

'Oh, Milo,' Sarah-Louise snapped, 'forget all that nonsense. Just get on with it. That's what everyone else is doing. Sure, Pummelcrush is mean, but he is a genius!'

Milo knew she wasn't really cross with him. She was his friend. Still, he found it annoying.

'Fine. I'll get on with things,' he said, deciding to keep his mouth shut and do his own investigating.

'Sarah-Louise is probably right – the whole country can't be wrong,' said Katie. 'Now, everyone, chill out with a disgusting spoon of nutri-paste and let's relax before we hit the books.'

Milo rolled his eyes and lifted a spoonful of sludge.

Chapter 5

The surest way to corrupt a youth is
to instruct him to hold in higher esteem
those who think alike than
those who think differently.
– Friedrich Nietzsche

The next few days passed without event. Milo began to think that he might have miraculously escaped punishment. *Maybe the Disciplods are embarrassed that I gave them the slip*, he thought.

Until an announcement was made: *Student 8728473, Milo Moloney, meet Mrs Agnes Gurney, today; 5.30pm.*

Milo felt his stomach drop. He had heard rumours of Mrs Gurney. She was Pummelcrush's most trusted adviser. The only person besides the Disciplods that he was ever seen talking to.

When the time arrived, two Disciplods appeared in the canteen as if from nowhere.

'Come with us,' they said. Before Milo had a chance to reply, they lifted him out of the seat and dragged him to the exit, the toes of his shoes trailing the shiny floor.

'Is this really necessary?' asked Milo, struggling to get free.

There was no answer, only a tightening of their grip.

They arrived at Mrs Gurney's office. The Disciplods clicked their watches and the door opened.

Bright, blinding lamps shone down from the ceiling giving the room a clinical feel. There was a big metal desk on one side and a long white hospital bed on the other. The walls were covered with screens that showed every angle of the school campus alongside all sorts of graphs and charts, updating in real time.

Agnes Gurney stood in the centre of the room with a clipboard under her arm. She was a strange-looking woman. She had flat, straight, dark-brown hair that fell to her shoulders. Her fringe came down to her eyebrows and made a perfect line across her forehead. She wore square, red-framed glasses that reflected the lamplight, obscuring her eyes. She had bright-red lipstick and a bright-red blazer. All of this gave her a severe and angular look.

'Place him on the bed – and use the straps this time,' she ordered, ignoring Milo.

'The straps? What?' Milo asked, panic setting in. 'What's going on?'

'Quiet.'

'But why? I'm not a prisoner!'

She stopped and looked up. 'Don't worry, Mr Moloney. This is just a precautionary measure. We must protect ourselves in case you have another outburst while we examine you.'

'Protect yourself?' said Milo. 'Against *me*?'

The Disciplods strapped him forcefully to the bed, thick leather straps tight around his wrists and ankles.

'Yes,' said Mrs Gurney matter-of-factly. 'You're here because of your disruptive behaviour. We must safeguard ourselves while we investigate the root cause.'

'But I was –'

'Shh, now,' she cut him off without even looking at him. 'You will speak when spoken to.'

He heard someone else enter.

'This is Professor Borlington from StifleCorp.'

Milo lay on his back, his body completely restrained. He could move his head, but all he could see in the bright lights were two imposing shadow-like figures peering over him.

'So, this is the subject?' Professor Borlington spoke in a gruff voice, like she had been smoking cigarettes all her life. 'Doesn't look like much.'

'Yes. Male. Thirteen years old. Recent temper flare-up in class where he was ejected for questioning both the authority of the instructor and the school system.'

'Hmm, sounds like a case of oppositional defiance disorder,' said Professor Borlington. 'I can't stand these ones.'

'Yes, classic ODD,' responded the icy-cold Gurney. 'I'm surprised he was accepted at all.'

'Eh, hello?' said Milo. 'I can hear everything you are saying.'

There was no response.

'There is nothing wrong with me. I don't have a disorder. I can explain all of those things if you would let me.'

'You see? Remarkable. Even now he continues to oppose and defy authority,' Gurney said, continuing to ignore Milo.

Every time Milo was ignored or talked down to, it was like he shrank, smaller and smaller, while the world and people around him grew and grew. Right now he felt the size of a tiny mouse, and Gurney and Borlington were colossal. Being dismissed like this made him feel weak and powerless. And angry. It was exactly the opposite of how he felt when he talked with Ursula.

'I'm just trying to explain,' Milo persisted.

'Shh, quiet, we're not here to punish you. We are here to *understand* you, so we can cure you. You should be grateful to have this opportunity to be fixed. You know how many children would give anything to be in your position?'

The bed was wheeled out from the wall. Borlington and Gurney stood on either side of Milo, the lamp light shining directly into his eyes.

He could smell cigarettes off Borlington's breath. This, mixed with Gurney's sickeningly sweet perfume, made him nauseous.

'Yes, boy,' said Borlington, 'don't be afraid. Think of it like you have a disease. You have a disorder. But we can help.'

'I don't have any of those things,' snapped Milo. 'I just got in a bit of trouble in school. It's pretty normal.'

'Ha! You are anything but normal,' said Borlington.

'Fascinating, the level of denial,' said Gurney. 'Let's go through the check-list. Were you disruptive in class recently?'

'Well, yes, but –'

'Yes or no is fine,' said Borlington.

'Do you have a problem with authority?' Gurney went on.

'Sometimes, yes, but it's not –'

'Just answer the questions!' snapped Gurney. 'Do you have a problem following rules?'

'Not always.'

'But sometimes?'

'Sometimes, yes.'

'I'll put that as a yes.'

'Do you distract other students from their work?'

'Not on purpose. But yes,' Milo answered sheepishly.

'Do you realise what you are doing when you disrupt the class?' Gurney asked, her voice getting angry. 'Do you have any idea what it means to the other students to be here? Do you know what it means to their parents? The sacrifices they have made. And your parents too. Do you think they would be proud of your behaviour?'

'I never thought of it like that.' He felt tiny, on the verge of disappearing.

'No, you didn't. Disordered students never do,' Borlington hissed.

'Well, we know what your parents think. They were informed. They've written a note. Shall I read it?'

'Something tells me you are going to.'

'Yes. I am.'

Dear Milo,

We are very disappointed to hear about your disruptive behaviour. We have sacrificed so much to send you to the Institute. Don't waste this opportunity. Please do as Mrs Gurney and Dr Pummelcrush say. Just put your head down and work hard.

With love,

Mam and Dad

Milo felt a sob rising up through his chest. It was hard to hear his parents' disappointment.

'What do you have to say?' asked Gurney.

'I dunno, I'm sorry. But my friend was sick –'

'We're not interested in your excuses. It's far too late for that.'

'We've also kept a record of every eye-roll, grimace and shake of your head that you've made,' said Gurney. 'You clearly have a problem with taking instruction and respecting authority.'

'But that doesn't mean I'm abnormal, does it?'

'I'm afraid so. Most students appreciate this opportunity. But not you,' Gurney continued. 'No – you want to be …' she paused and looked at her notes, 'a musician? Good grief. You must grow up and stop acting so childish. Stop fantasising and get real. You do realise you made a commitment to be here. You signed a pledge. Are you going to break your promise?'

Milo was tired and confused, and he was getting a headache. It felt like he had been answering questions for ages.

'The question is what to do with you and your ODD,' she said to herself. They began talking to each other, as if he wasn't there.

'Could he be a good candidate for processing?' Gurney asked Borlington.

'I don't think so. Nothing would give me greater pleasure than processing this one. But the contraption is not ready. He is still too challenging.'

'Isn't that the whole point? To cure these types of troublemakers?'

'Yes, but these types take longer to process.'

'When?' asked Gurney impatiently. 'We were promised it would be ready this year, in time for the rankings.'

'I can't say. This is a serious device with serious implications. It can't be rushed. Dr Pummelcrush will have to be patient.'

'You know as well as I do that is not one of his strong suits.'

Milo's mind clouded over in a dark fog; did he really have oppositional defiance disorder?

He did feel different sometimes. But not abnormal. Then he thought of Ursula and their conversations. How she listened with genuine interest to what he said. She'd told him that asking questions, challenging authority is not always bad. It was important. It was philosophy.

This thought settled his anxiety for a moment. He tuned in to what they were saying.

'It works on the weaker ones. But it takes much longer to work on the strong-minded ones.'

'Well, Dr Pummelcrush is not going to be happy,' snapped Gurney.

'I'm sorry, but we are not going to use the contraption unless we are sure it's ready,' replied Borlington. 'We have a reputation to protect too.'

'Don't talk to me about your reputation. You do understand what is at stake this year? It's the world number one ranking.'

'We are working round the clock, I promise.'

'Just do it.' Gurney turned back to Milo. 'As for you, take this as a warning. If you don't learn to do what you are told, you will fail, not only here, but in life. To reach your true potential, to unleash your excellence, takes discipline, sacrifice and surrender. For your own sake, do what you are told and stop asking questions. Otherwise, the consequences will be dire. Do you understand me?'

'Yes, Mrs Gurney,' answered Milo politely.

'Now the first step is admitting you have a problem. So repeat after me: "I have a disorder. I am not normal. I must get better."'

Milo, blinded, confused and exhausted, just wanted to get away, so he repeated the lines: 'I have a disorder. I am not normal. I must get better.'

The Disciplods unclasped the thick leather restraints and hoisted him off the bed. Milo rubbed his wrists as they marched him out of the office and let him loose in the hallway.

'You must proceed to study hall immediately or you will be late. Also, fix your uniform. It is not perfect.' The Disciplod pointed to Milo's rolled-up sleeves.

Milo, in no mood for being further demeaned, snapped back. 'Neither is yours.' He reached up and flicked the Disciplod's tie out over his jumper.

The Disciplod checked his tie, and Milo gave him a tiny flick on the chin.

His expression never changed but he began to move towards Milo.

Milo pointed behind the Disciplod: 'Uh-oh! It's our esteemed leader Dr Pummelcrush. All hail! He looks mad at you.'

The Disciplod turned sharply, and Milo skipped off in the other direction out of sight.

But as he was leaving, he saw another door just down the hallway, slightly ajar. He could hear murmurings. He was angry, and he was curious to find out what they were talking about. He peered through the door, but jumped back when he saw a student floating and rotating in mid-air.

Milo realised that the voice he was hearing was the soft, patronising tones of Du-Ped. And it seemed to be caught on a loop. When he looked again, he saw that it wasn't a real person: it was a hologram. It was a rotating hologram of a student, alternating between male and female. Beside the image was a list of words in boxes. It looked like an image from his biology notes. Yet instead of outlining the attributes of the anatomy, this named ideal Institute students' characteristics:

- Obedient
- Manageable
- Unflappable
- Efficient
- Focused
- Dependable

When he looked again, he could hear the Du-Ped voice clearly, as the hologram changed from a student to the Institute campus to images of thousands of people working in a factory.

Experience our latest advance in human resources.
A hyper-efficient system for creating the perfect workers.
Ideal for military, manufacturing or technical professions.
Our workers do not ask for time off or for raises, they
never quit, and they do not go on strike. Contact: Agnes
Gurney for more information.

Milo stood with his mouth and eyes wide open. The voice sounded like a TV ad, or a sales pitch. But – for *students*? Then the tone changed, became more excited:

Coming soon! The REDUCON 6000: a ground-
breaking device designed to process more students faster,
transforming them into the most loyal and efficient
workers ever. Contact: Agnes Gurney.

What the hell? he thought. *Could that be the device that Gurney and Borlington were talking about?*

He heard Borlington and Gurney leaving the office. He darted down the corridor to the study hall as fast as he could, arriving just on time.

Milo didn't say a word to anyone. Katie and Sarah-Louise wouldn't believe him, yet. He had no actual proof, plus he wasn't sure what it all meant.

All night his mind raced: the hologram, the sales pitch, the processing that Borlington and Gurney mentioned.

What is going on here? He was sure that whatever it was, it was something bad.

He had to talk to Ursula. She was the only one who might listen and take him seriously.

Chapter 6

To live without philosophising
is in truth the same as keeping the eyes closed
without attempting to open them.
– René Descartes

Milo went to see Ursula the next day. The students had one free study-hall period every second Friday, and this was a free-period Friday. He checked to make sure the corridor was clear before entering the garden. He spotted Ursula sitting reading.

'Hi, Milo,' she said. 'I was just thinking about you. We should say that you are helping me with some vegetable-growing when you visit, in case anyone asks.'

'Will they believe that?'

'Oh, I'm sure. I used to have loads of volunteers, but they've dwindled now. No-one pays me much attention anyway, so we should be fine. Are you OK? You seem a bit down.'

'I got examined by Mrs Gurney and Professor Borlington yesterday.'

'Examined? Why? What did they find?'

'They think I have oppositional defiance disorder. They said there is something wrong with me. That's why I get in trouble.' Milo hung his head.

'That's outrageous,' said Ursula defiantly, getting up from her seat. 'Pure nonsense. You are a healthy, bright, sensitive, energetic boy! Don't listen to a word those boring bullies say.'

'I don't feel like there is anything wrong with me.'

'Of course there isn't! I've been teaching young people for many years. You are totally fine, Milo. Do not let that kind of talk get into your head. They are trying to make you feel bad about yourself, so you'll surrender to them and their system for security.'

'But why do I get in more trouble than other students?'

'You get into trouble, Milo, because you have the soul of a philosopher. You like to question things. You want to know why things are the way they are. And that's a good thing. That's how all the change and progress in human history has happened!'

'It is?'

'Yes. What if we never questioned the way things were done? What if we never had any brave people to show us things could be different, could be better? We would still be stuck in a time of barbarism, cruelty, slavery and oppression. Women wouldn't be able to vote, children would be working in factories, people would still own slaves. The only way things can get better is when someone asks why things have to be this way, why can't they be different?'

'It's hard to feel that sometimes, though,' said Milo.

'It's so hard, Milo. Those in power always want to keep power, and they will do anything to hang on to it. But their most dangerous weapon is not armies or police forces.

It's controlling ideas. It's making people believe that things can't be different.

Just then, Milo remembered what he had come to talk to Ursula about. He explained about the 'processing' that Gurney and Borlington talked about, and the hologram and sales pitch.

'Hmm ... that is strange,' Ursula said. 'Could it be some kind of marketing campaign, to help the students get jobs?'

'Maybe, but I'm sure it said something about placing an order. And then there was this REDUCON thing. Some kind of fancy new technology that makes students obedient and efficient.'

'Just like the Disciplods,' Ursula said.

'Exactly. Ursula, I do not want to end up like them.'

'No, of course not.'

'So, what do you think?' asked Milo.

'I'm really not sure. If they are actually selling students, then this is a serious criminal operation.'

'Should we tell someone?'

'It's too early yet, I think,' Ursula said. 'Let's make a note of it for now and try to find out more.'

'OK,' said Milo, a little disappointed. He wanted action, and maybe some revenge. He trusted Ursula, but he could see she was still a little afraid of Dr Pummelcrush.

'You know, Milo, if they are trying to make more Disciplods, I think philosophy might help you.'

'What do you mean? How can philosophy help?'

'Well,' said Ursula, 'doing philosophy is the opposite of being a passive robot – it's all about challenging, questioning and actively using your mind to figure out what is right or wrong, true or false. It doesn't tell you to accept whatever you are told. It encourages you to think for yourself.'

'Well, then, let's do more of it!' said Milo. 'The last thing I ever want is to end up like a Disciplod, having to take orders from Pummelcrush all day. Eugh.'

'Yes, let's! Also, Milo, I've been thinking. I think that the best way to learn philosophy is through conversation. I'm not interested in standing here and lecturing you. You spend enough time being told what to think, right?'

'For sure.'

'So that is how we will do philosophy together, through conversations. And I had an idea for our next one! Are you ready?'

'Yes!'

URSULA: You mentioned earlier about the technology in the school. So, I want to ask you a philosophical question to start off: do you think technology is good for us?

MILO: Yes, of course. Technology is great.

URSULA: Why do you think that?

MILO: Because people use their phones, laptops, computers all the time to make things easier. Sometimes I wonder how people lived before technology.

URSULA: You think technology is a modern thing? That we are the first people to have technology?

MILO: Yeah – obviously – technology is the newest thing. My dad always talks about how when he was young, they didn't have all this technology.

URSULA: And yet he seemed to get on OK, didn't he?

MILO: Ha, that's what he says too. But it must have been harder, not having the internet and not being able to do all the things we can do.

URSULA: Like what?

MILO: Like, I dunno, say you're out and you need to get home, you can just text your mam to ask her to collect you. Or if you are struggling with homework, you can look it up online. People in the olden days couldn't do that.

URSULA: That's true. But let's get clear on something: what exactly is technology?

MILO: Easy. Technology is, like, phones and laptops and computers and stuff.

URSULA: OK, so what do all those things have in common?

MILO: They are all communication-type things. Like they help you communicate … and find stuff out … and you can play games on them. So they're fun. Is that right?

URSULA: It's certainly not wrong. We are exploring tricky questions so exactly what is right is difficult to know. You said technology is for communication, to find stuff out and for fun, right?

MILO: Yeah, something like that.

URSULA: Well, then what about books? Couldn't you say books fit that description? And therefore books are technology?

MILO: Books? *What?* Nooooooo! A book is like the very opposite of technology.

URSULA: Why?

MILO: I'm not sure how to explain it, but … like, a book doesn't light up or beep and you don't plug it in to charge it.

URSULA: But does it not help you find things out? Is it not fun sometimes? And can it not be used for communication?

MILO: I mean, yeah, you can find stuff out and enjoy it, but you can't use it to call your mam!

URSULA (laughing): That may be true, but that doesn't mean it doesn't communicate. Didn't someone write the book? Isn't the author communicating with us?

MILO: Ahhh. I never thought of that. But, yeah, it does. The author is communicating with all the people who read it. Kind of like a group chat. When you send a message out to lots of people at once.

URSULA: Yes, exactly!

MILO: Wait, are we saying now that a book is technology? Because that just seems weird to me.

URSULA: Sure, why not? It's something we have invented to help us to communicate and share information. And remember, philosophy is about keeping an open mind.

MILO: OK, fine. But I just thought technology was electric or powered, you know?

URSULA: Yes, I understand – but maybe that's just modern technology. Think back to your dad – were there other things he had that we could call technology?

MILO: Hmm, let me see. Oh, the TV, fridge, camera, microwave, washing machine, cars? Are they technology?

URSULA: I would say so, yes. But, besides the TV, they don't really help you to look things up, have fun or communicate, do they?

MILO: I guess not.

URSULA: So if it's not limited to communication, then what makes something technology?

Milo tapped his fingers on his chin. It was exhilarating to think this way after having to listen to Pummelcrush throw facts at them for so long.

MILO: Well, all those things we make to help us to do things we want to do in a faster way, that we couldn't do ourselves.

URSULA: Good – I like that. That could be a definition: technology is things made by humans that help us to do things we want to do more efficiently.

MILO: Seems about right. But that means a lot of things are technology.

URSULA: Like what?

MILO: Well – planes, boats, cars, buses, bikes, and then clothes and houses, and everything we have made to help us to do things.

URSULA: Yes, why not – what's the difference between

a computer and a road? Don't both require our knowledge to turn material from the earth into something we can use to help us to do something we want to do?

MILO: Yes, that's true. But a computer is much more complicated than a road.

URSULA: It's true that as we get more knowledge about the world, we are capable of creating more complex and powerful technologies. From simple tools like hammers and wheels, to something as big and complex as the internet. But they are all a series of attempts to extend our powers over the world.

MILO: Hmm. I never thought that there could be so much to think about technology.

It was happening again. The conversation with Ursula was really starting to stir Milo's imagination. He imagined himself and Ursula flying above the Earth, hurtling back through time. In his mind's eye, he could see the first humans picking up a rock to use as a tool. He saw first the invention of the wheel, then roads, carts, spears, guns, trains, factories, hospitals, and so on up to computers, smartphones, drone-balls and lasers. *This philosophy business really changes your perspective*, he thought. *It gives you a sense of time on a way bigger scale. It's as if you can look at humanity from above.* Weird but wonderful!

URSULA: But remember, the original question was whether it is good for us or not. Technology, I mean.

MILO: Well, clearly it is. I mean, we just listed all the things it has helped us to do, right?

URSULA: Yes – it definitely allows us to do more things. But is that always for the better?

MILO: Well, for the most part, yeah, I think so.

URSULA: Are there examples of technologies that have made things worse?

MILO: Well, guns and bombs – all those things we made that have only led to death and destruction. They might increase our powers, but that can be bad too.

URSULA: Very good point, Milo. Technology can be used for bad as well as good.

MILO: Yeah, and then, think of medicine – that has been so good for people, helping them live longer and healthier.

URSULA: Right – so we have the bad, the good and everything in between. Doesn't really answer our original question, does it?

MILO: Not really. But I think I've a better understanding of it now.

URSULA: What do you mean?

MILO: Well, the question was, 'Is technology good for us?' And maybe there is no simple answer. I'm starting to think that technology is neither good nor bad in itself. It's people. It's how we use it. You can use a hammer to build a house for someone or hit them on the head.

URSULA: Excellent.

MILO: And you can use your phone to call your friend to cheer them up, or to bully someone by being mean. The phone is just a thing we can use any way we want.

URSULA: That's an excellent observation. A wise thought, young man.

MILO: Although I suppose some technologies kind of force you to act in certain ways.

URSULA: What do you mean?

MILO: Well, there is not much good you can do with a bomb.

URSULA: That's true.

MILO: So, maybe it's not just how we use it, but how it's designed and made?

URSULA: I never really thought of it that way, but you're right; tools are not completely neutral; how they are designed can encourage us towards certain ways of acting.

'And now, it's time for dinner, Milo,' said Ursula. 'But that was really great – you see how we explored the question, played around with the ideas and came out without a clear answer, but a better understanding?'

'Absolutely – and it was fun!'

Milo hopped up and grabbed his bag and was heading for the door. 'I was thinking, can I bring some friends with me some time?'

'I don't know about that, Milo. It's risky enough as it is.'

'Not if we say we're volunteering for the vegetable garden?'

'Hmm, OK. Let's give it another few sessions and then maybe.'

'OK! I know who I'll ask already ... I'll have to convince them first.'

'Now run before you get in trouble.'

Milo made his way quickly to the canteen.

Chapter 7

Doubt is not a pleasant condition,
but certainty is an absurd one.
– Voltaire

'Good morning, students. We have some wonderful news as we continue to march on our path that will take us towards the direction of excellence.'

Milo resisted the urge to roll his eyes in case they might actually fall back into his head. He was with Liam and Gerry, Katie and Sarah-Louise, eating their gloopy breakfast. He could tell Liam and Gerry shared his cynical feelings about the morning announcements.

'This week we have special VIP visits from world leaders, including the Prime Minister of China. Our partners at StifleCorp will be reviewing progress on the new east wing. The Disciplods will be sitting pre-exams for the State Licensed Assessment Metrics, the SLAMs. We wish these brave warriors the very best. We're counting on you. In other news ...'

And on it went. Du-Ped listed off all the wonderful and amazing things happening in the school. The picture painted by Du-Ped was in such stark contrast to Milo's daily experience that it was difficult to believe it was the same school.

'Where's Paul Patrick?' Milo asked, noticing that his friend wasn't in the canteen. Milo felt protective of him since that time he was to blame for Paul Patrick's first butt-shock.

'Dunno,' answered Liam, wolfing down his third bowl of sludge. 'Sick maybe?'

'He wasn't in class yesterday either,' said Gerry.

'Huh, weird,' Katie said, as she twisted her long curls.

'I didn't even notice, to be honest,' said Sarah-Louise, who was reviewing her notes for this week's quiz. She was so proud of her award-winning notes.

'Me neither until now,' said Milo. 'Maybe he got some sense and escaped.'

'Milo, shh!' said Sarah-Louise, as the others stifled a giggle, always cautious of nearby drone-balls hovering.

As they approached class, Milo could see Pummelcrush and Gurney speaking in hushed tones.

All Milo could hear was, 'I've waited long enough. You have the test subject. Now begin the process!'

Then Pummelcrush stormed off, leaving Gurney looking visibly upset. It was weird to see her show emotion. She caught Milo's eye and quickly straightened herself out, becoming stiff and angular once more.

They entered class. Pummelcrush glared across the room, squinting at each student. Nobody dared move a muscle. Pummelcrush grunted. 'The International Ranking Committee will arrive here in a matter of months. And we still have little snotty brats failing quizzes.'

What is he on about? thought Milo.

'We must do better.' It was as if he was speaking to

himself. 'We must be number one! You!' He pointed his baton at Consuela in the front row. 'Stop breathing so heavily. You're driving me insane. Did your parents not teach you to breathe properly?'

She sat there unsure of what to do. So she held her breath until he moved on.

'Now, on with the lesson plan.'

Once again, the class braced themselves for an onslaught of facts, figures and rules to memorise and regurgitate.

For the next few days, there was no sign of Paul Patrick. This was strange. People were never absent for this long.

Milo was worried. He knew Paul Patrick wasn't the strongest kid around. Milo was itching to report his disappearance to Ursula.

But the next day, without a word of explanation, Paul Patrick was back in class. As Milo entered, he saw him standing directly beside Pummelcrush and staring up at him.

'Shine my shoes,' Pummelcrush snapped.

Without hesitation, Paul Patrick was down on all fours, using the sleeve of his uniform to shine Pummelcrush's flawless black leather brogues.

'Good boy, very good,' said Pummelcrush, as if talking to a dog. 'Now go to your seat, sit and focus. You understand?'

'Yes, Dr Pummelcrush. I will not fail you. I am proud to serve you.'

Straight away Milo noticed how Paul Patrick's walk was different. He always walked on his toes, bouncing up and down. But now, his walk was stiff, flat and mechanical.

On first glance, it was the same red-haired, freckly kid, but there was something disturbingly different about him. Then Milo saw it. His once bright eyes had dimmed beyond recognition. All the light was gone. Paul Patrick had the brightest blue eyes. It was so noticeable because they stood out against his blazing red hair. Now his eyes were a dull grey, like someone turned down the colour setting. Whereas before his eyes had darted around, anxious and aware, now they were still, locked onto Dr Pummelcrush. His hands lay flat on the desk and his legs, usually hopping up and down with nervous energy, were motionless.

Throughout the day, Pummelcrush kept glancing to check on Paul Patrick, and he would smile a little every time.

When the bell rang, Milo signalled to Sarah-Louise and Katie for them to follow his lead. They waited outside the classroom until Paul Patrick came out.

The floor moved and they were on their way down through the school to the canteen.

'Hey, Paul Patrick, how's things?' Milo asked, as casually as he could.

'I am excellent, thank you. I feel one hundred per cent. I am on a path to unleash my excellence and reach my potential.' Paul Patrick's voice was robotic.

Milo shot Sarah-Louise a concerned look. 'Riiiiight, yeeeeeah. I guess that's pretty cool. Where have you been the last few days?'

'I received a special educational treatment here at the Institute to help me on my path to success. The Secondary Training Institute for Lifelong Employment is the greatest school in the world,' he replied, each word delivered in the same stilted, awkward rhythm.

His eyes were pointed at Milo, but they were looking through him – just like the Disciplods'.

Sarah-Louise and Katie shrugged their shoulders.

'Uh huh,' replied Milo. 'Where exactly?'

'The Institute is perfectly equipped to guide young students in their needs for the twenty-first century,' Paul Patrick continued.

Consuela Petherbridge, who was standing right in front of them, turned her head. She looked concerned.

Milo looked at her and shook his head.

Without making a sound, Consuela mouthed: 'What's up with him?'

Katie, Sarah-Louise and Milo just shrugged and shook their heads.

Milo was getting impatient. 'Yes, but you were missing for three days.'

Sarah-Louise shot him a look. 'Paul Patrick, don't mind Milo, he is just being rude. Hey, remember when I puked on Pummelcrush? That was pretty funny, wasn't it?' she said, taking a different approach. She remembered Paul Patrick's infectious giggle – maybe she could make him laugh.

Paul Patrick just stared ahead. 'Misbehaving is wasteful and a distraction. We must focus if we are to be part of the greatest school in the world.'

Consuela shook her head and locked eyes with Sarah-Louise.

The way he spoke was horrifying and bewildering. It was like there was a little tape recorder inside his head repeating certain sentences. When asked a question, he had to wait a moment for the operator to choose the right one, and then he had to complete the thought from start to finish.

Katie tried one more tactic. 'Oh, I forgot to take notes for that last lesson. Can you send me yours? I'll owe you one!'

'It is against the rules to share notes,' he said. 'We each must take responsibility for ourselves. The Institute is an elite school. We are lucky to be here.'

Milo shook his head and whispered: 'What have they done to you?'

'This is pointless,' Katie said.

'See?' said Milo. 'I told you this place is not right. It's like he is brainwashed.'

'He reminds me of the Disciplods,' Consuela whispered.

'Hmm,' said Sarah-Louise, 'this is very strange.'

From that point on, the atmosphere around the school changed. It became more fraught and intense.

The next week, another student, Vanessa Del Poitro, was taken out of study hall for blowing her nose too loudly. She wasn't back in class for two days. When she returned she was just like Paul Patrick, a robotic zombie drone.

The week after that, another two students were removed from the canteen for taking too long to finish their bowl of nutri-paste.

And another student, that same day, was given detention for yawning during Pummelcrush's lesson.

None of them was seen around the school for a few days.

And then, they all returned like zombies, but really boring zombies, who, rather than feast on the brains of the living, wanted just to heap praise on the school every chance they got.

Milo approached each one. All had become obedient and lifeless. Just as the hologram had advertised. They all had the same dead eyes, the same stiff walk and singular focus, like the Disciplods.

They followed Pummelcrush around like a swarm of flies. He was obsessed with them, pointing them out as shining examples of how to behave. He took perverse pleasure in ordering them around. It made him despise the other students even more.

Pummelcrush was at best a cantankerous task master, but since these zombie-robots showed up, it was like he was looking for any excuse to punish students.

Blink too often. Detention.

Sneeze too loudly. Detention.

Have a weird walk. Detention.

Fear spread through the school. Who was going to be next?

But Milo wasn't going to wait around to find out. It was time to become proactive. He wasn't sure exactly what to do, but he was determined, even if he had to do it on his own.

Chapter 8

Attention is the rarest and purest form of generosity.
— Simone Weil

Any chance he got, Milo went to talk to Ursula. These visits kept him sane while people were on edge. Ursula usually had some topic prepared. One day they talked about whether people are free to do what they want to do.

URSULA: We think we are free, Milo, but do you think it could be that our futures are limited or even pre-destined ... already 'written'?

MILO: I've always felt free. If I decide to lift my arm I feel it's my decision. And I feel I could make different decisions if I wanted to.

URSULA: But you can't decide to do just *anything*, can you?

MILO: Well, I dunno, maybe not. I mean, I guess I can't do just *anything*. I can't fly and I'd probably never make it as a professional boxer ... too small and weak. And let's be honest, I doubt I'd have the smarts to be a brain surgeon. So I'm not *totally* free to do whatever I want. Humans are limited, and some people are even more limited than others. But I still

think I can choose and decide *some* things for myself.
Like wave my arm like this.

URSULA: OK, I get you. But would you agree that
everything in the world has a cause? Something that
came before it that led to it?

MILO: Yes, I think so.

URSULA: Well, if everything that happens in the world
has a cause, if everything is the result of something
that happened before, then wouldn't that mean even
your 'decisions' were caused by what came before?
And then they weren't free, but just the next event in
a chain that goes back and back?

MILO: I think I understand, but it feels in my mind
like I just made that decision of my own free will
right now.

URSULA: There is no denying it feels like that, but I
mean really you just waved your arm because this
conversation caused you to make a philosophical
point. Aren't all our decisions just caused by whatever
came before?

MILO: OK, now, this is a tricky one.

Another day they talked about whether it is always better
to have more knowledge.

URSULA: Is there a limit to the value of knowledge, do
you think, Milo?

MILO: No, I don't think so. The more you know, the
better.

URSULA: Why do you say that, Milo?

MILO: Well, knowledge helps you to solve problems, to make better decisions and to understand the world, doesn't it? All good things!

URSULA: I'm not so sure that's always the case, though. Would you like to know, for example, what your friends thought about you at all times?

MILO: Hmm, maybe not.

URSULA: Or would you want to know if existence was truly meaningless? Or would you like to know the date of your own death?

MILO: Hmm, maybe not those things either. No.

URSULA: So, would you agree that it's sometimes better not to know? Sometimes perhaps there is wisdom in choosing not to know, or at least, choosing what is worth knowing.

MILO: But isn't wisdom the same as knowledge?

URSULA: For me, wisdom is much more important, Milo, and much more difficult to attain, than knowledge.

MILO: Explain, please! What do you mean by 'wisdom'?

URSULA: wisdom is about integrating your knowledge, your feelings, your emotions, in the service of living a good and happy life.

MILO: I see, yes. It's about how you use your knowledge?

URSULA: That's it. Wisdom is about having good judgement and making good decisions.

MILO: You know, Ursula, you seem pretty wise to me!

These conversations gave Milo a sense of being heard. Now he came to think of it, he noticed how rare that was. Even his parents didn't always pay attention when he was talking to them, which was very frustrating. And as for the teachers at this school! He might as well not have a voice at all. But with Ursula it was different. It was so energising to have someone really hear what he had to say, for a change.

The time came for Milo to invite Katie and Sarah-Louise to join them. He was delighted with their reaction when he took them to the philosophy garden.

'Wow,' said Katie, 'this place is so pretty!' She twirled around the garden smelling flowers and touching the trees.

'It's beautiful,' said Sarah-Louise, wide-eyed, but cautious. 'But are you sure we won't get in trouble?'

'Don't worry,' said Ursula. 'This is about as safe as you are going to get in this school. I've sent a message to the principal, saying I've started a small gardening group. That's you three!'

Milo had told Ursula about how kids were disappearing and reappearing as zombies. He said he thought they should tell someone about what was going on.

'Take it easy, Milo,' said Sarah-Louise. 'We don't know anything for sure. Maybe they just had intense lessons for a few days and decided to knuckle down, like sensible students.'

'Something is not right,' said Ursula, 'but still, we don't have any evidence just yet, so let's not rush into anything.'

Milo groaned impatiently, but he didn't argue.

'Anyway, that's not why you're here,' said Ursula. 'Katie and Sarah-Louise, tell me what you know about philosophy.'

'Not much,' replied Katie, still wandering, admiring the flowers, 'but I like the sound of it.'

'Just the few bits Milo has told us,' said Sarah-Louise. 'The thing I don't get is how there are no clear right and wrong answers. How can that be?'

'It's not that there are no right and wrong answers,' said Ursula. 'There may well be. It's more that for some important questions, there are no easy, simple answers. But that shouldn't stop us from trying to find out!'

'What kind of important questions?' asked Sarah-Louise.

Milo wasn't surprised that Sarah-Louise was suspicious of philosophy. For her, the world was black and white, right or wrong, true or false. She didn't have much patience for the grey areas, the uncertainties. From what he understood, philosophy spent a lot of time in those areas.

'Well, things like these,' said Ursula. 'What is the right way to live? How do we know what is true and what is false? Did the universe have a cause? These are important but difficult questions, and they don't have simple, easy answers. But, how about we take an easier example to start off? Let's take one that we all probably have thought about: whether it is right or wrong to eat meat.'

URSULA: Do you eat meat?

Milo and Sarah-Louise both nodded.

URSULA: So, then you must think it's OK to hurt animals for our own pleasure?

MILO: No, I wouldn't put it like that. It's not for pleasure but out of need.

URSULA: Do you need to eat chicken and beef every day? You know that in order for you to eat meat thousands of animals need to be raised, kept and killed every day.

SARAH-LOUISE: OK, maybe not *need*, but it's normal and natural for us to eat meat.

MILO: Plus, aren't we just the top of the food chain? We have always eaten meat.

URSULA: Are you saying it's OK because we have always done it?'

MILO: Well, no, I don't think that's a good reason.

URSULA: Well, then are you saying it's OK because we are more powerful than animals? We're the best hunters?

MILO: Yeah, I guess so. Something like that.

URSULA: So the strongest or most powerful is justified in hurting and using the weaker for their own desires?

MILO: Hmm, I know I haven't thought this through, but for the sake of the discussion, I'll say yes.

URSULA: Well, then, what's to stop the strongest country from invading a weaker one and eating the people? Or a stronger group of friends beating up a weaker group and keeping them as slaves?

SARAH-LOUISE: It's different between humans. I don't think the same rules apply.

URSULA: Why?

SARAH-LOUISE: Humans are a separate species. It just feels more wrong for us to kill another human than to kill a chicken.

URSULA: So we can kill and use things as long as they are not from our species?

SARAH-LOUISE (doubtfully): I suppose so.

URSULA (laughing): Don't worry, this is not a trap – we are just following your points to their logical conclusion. We are exploring ideas.

MILO: Let's keep doing that!

URSULA: So, you've separated the world by species. Our species gets treated one way; other species get treated another way. Correct?

SARAH-LOUISE: Correct.

URSULA: But how is that any different from separating the world by nationality, or race or religion?'

SARAH-LOUISE: What do you mean?

Milo could see Sarah-Louise was becoming more and more interested in the twists and turns of philosophical discussion. Katie, meanwhile, still wandered the garden. She had put a flower in her hair, but she was listening.

URSULA: I mean, you have picked a category – species – to decide who it's OK to kill. But why? Why not colour, or where you're from, or if you're a boy or a girl?

SARAH-LOUISE: Well, it's definitely wrong to treat people differently based on any of those things.

URSULA: Oh, I agree, but then why is it OK to treat animals differently?

SARAH-LOUISE: I think I see your point, but I think humans are just – special, you know. It just seems like such a different thing to harm a human versus harming an animal – even though I don't think it's good to harm animals for no reason.

URSULA: In what way are humans so special?

SARAH-LOUISE: We are smarter, more intelligent.

MILO: Yes. We know more. We can talk and tell each other to stop doing things. We can build cities and planes and all these things.

URSULA: OK, well, then it's not really about species: it's about intelligence and language?

MILO: Well, yeah, I think that is one of the main things at least. It would be hard to just kill something that could talk and reason with you and ask you to stop. Animals can't do that.

URSULA: OK, but some animals are pretty smart. Dolphins and ravens can solve puzzles, and chimpanzees can use sign language. Does that mean those animals should be exempt?

MILO: Maybe, but that doesn't feel right either.

URSULA: And what makes you so sure we are more intelligent anyway?

MILO: Well, look at all the stuff we can do and make, and we can trap animals and control them whenever we want.

URSULA: Doing things just because we can is hardly intelligent.

MILO: Ah, come on, Ursula. We are definitely more intelligent – look at all the problems we have solved! We can go to space.

URSULA: Sure, we can build more complex machines and we can travel further, but why is that a more intelligent thing to do? What if it's more intelligent to just sit back, eat, maybe have a family, enjoy life and die. What if our so called intelligence is the very thing that is going to end up resulting in the destruction of the whole environment?

SARAH-LOUISE: What do you mean? Like, climate change?

URSULA: Yes. We know for sure that because of our industries and technologies the natural environment has suffered greatly. Trees, rivers, the seas have all been destroyed, and the world might become unliveable soon because of the burning of fossil fuels, which powered all this innovation. Right?

SARAH-LOUISE: Yes, that's true.

URSULA: So the things you point to as the signs of our intelligence are the very things that may result in the destruction of our planet. Does that seem intelligent to you?

SARAH-LOUISE: I guess not.

URSULA: But maybe our intelligence will help us to solve the problems we face?

MILO: Maybe.

KATIE: So, I take it you think we should treat animals just the same as humans?

URSULA: Well, Katie, maybe not just the same. But I do wonder whether there is any good reason why we would knowingly cause suffering to creatures who can feel pain when it's not necessary. We don't need to eat meat. Why not give them a break?

KATIE: But, if we didn't eat meat, then there would be way less cows and pigs and sheep in the world. So many of them only exist because of us. Isn't that good?

URSULA: Hmm, interesting point. Farming does bring a lot of animals into the world that wouldn't exist otherwise. But, on the flip side, it's also responsible for polluting lakes, destroying forests, the destruction of biodiversity, of the habitats of insects and other animals, all to make way for cows and sheep.

MILO: I do wonder sometimes whether there are things we do now – like eating animals – that in a hundred or a thousand years will be looked on as being really awful.

URSULA: That's a very good question. What are the things we do today that will one day seem bad or wrong?

MILO: Treating children the way this school does!

URSULA (laughing): Quite possibly.

'But seriously,' said Sarah-Louise, 'do you think this school is actually a dangerous place for us?'

'I'll be honest, I have my doubts about this place,' said Ursula. 'But I'm still not sure what they are up to. Are they really selling students? Or are they just trying to educate them in their way and make sure they get jobs?'

'Is there a difference?' asked Milo.

'Perhaps not, Milo – but in the eyes of the law there would be.'

'What should we do?' asked Katie.

'Let's try and stay out of trouble,' said Sarah-Louise, 'keep our eyes peeled, and keep coming back here to do philosophy. You know, I really enjoyed that conversation. It was nice to think about something besides school, and it made me think about how we treat animals, but without telling me what to do, without pushing me to think in one way or the other.'

'That's great,' said Ursula. 'That is exactly what philosophy should do – open your mind to new possibilities and questions so you are in a better place to make decisions about what you believe and how you want to live. What about you, Katie? Did you enjoy it?'

'Oh, yes, I did. I thought it was really interesting. Thank you, Ursula.'

'And now we'd better go,' said Milo.

'Come back soon,' said Ursula, beginning to fill a bucket with fresh compost.

'We will,' said Katie, and Sarah-Louise waved.

They went out into the empty corridors. Only the constant distant hum of construction work could be heard.

'What's wrong with you?' Katie asked Milo. She was always sensitive to his moods.

'Don't you think we need to *do* something about what's going on?' said Milo.

'Do what, though, Milo?'

'*Tell* someone, fight back, find out what they are up to. I don't know. I enjoy the philosophy conversations, but we need to act!'

'Be patient, Milo,' said Sarah-Louise. 'We have to be careful. It could be dangerous.'

'I'm tired of being patient. Our friends are disappearing and coming back like dumb robots. I have to try and find out what's going on. You guys go ahead. I'm going to explore.'

'Milo, no, please,' said Sarah-Louise. 'Come with us.'

'No, I can't wait any longer.'

'Fine,' said Sarah-Louise. 'I'm not getting in trouble just because you can't wait,' and she stomped off in the direction of the dorms.

Katie just stood there, looking at Milo, unsure of which way to go.

'Go back, Katie! I'll be fine. I'll just take a quick look around.'

Then they heard the sound of footsteps approaching.

'Are you really sure you don't wanna come with us, Milo?' said Katie.

'Yes! Just go!' Milo walked away from her.

Katie was at the end of the corridor when Milo spotted two Disciplods barrelling around the corner. He ducked into a doorway and watched.

Horrified, he saw them freeze Katie's uniform and then pull her forcibly towards the restricted section.

Now what?

Milo didn't have much time to think, but he knew he had to see what was going on with Katie. He took off after them, silently, and followed them towards the restricted section of the school, where the new wing was under construction.

Chapter 9

The limits of tyrants are prescribed
by the endurance of those whom they oppress.
– Frederick Douglass

The Disciplods pushed past a large plastic sheet that covered an entire section of a corridor. There were signs everywhere with yellow and black striped tape criss-crossed in front:

Keep Out!
Under Construction!
New East Wing Coming Soon!

Milo thought the system must be tracking him, but he didn't care. He had to find out where they were taking Katie. So he pushed on in behind the plastic sheet through which the Disciplods had bundled her.

The air changed. A cool breeze blew past his face. It felt like outside.

The Disciplods were just a few metres ahead of him, getting into a lift, with Katie still struggling between them.

As soon as the lift doors closed, Milo ran up to it. It was travelling downwards – there was no upwards button – and he could hear that it was still in motion.

This was his only chance. He called the lift, and

eventually it came clanking up from the bowels of the building. In he got, and pressed B for basement. The lift went hurtling down into the unknown and landed with a thud.

When he got out, Milo was in a huge cave-like space, exposed rock arching high overhead. The temperature had dropped. There was a damp, slightly metallic smell of soil. The floor was covered in the same linoleum as the school. He had had no idea that there were these massive caves underneath the Institute.

He could hear faint sounds in the distance. He ran to take cover by the wall. He laid his hand on the cold rock and felt a thin film of wet slime. Tiny streams of water dribbled down the rock into drains that ran along the side of the floor on either side.

What is this place? he thought. *This does not look like it's going to be a new wing of the school. And what the hell has happened to Katie?*

He crept along the wall and reached a junction where the tunnel split into three. Pointing down one direction was a signpost saying: 'StifleCorp Headquarters'. Another said: 'Secondary Training Institute for Lifelong Employment' with an arrow pointing back the way he had come. Everyone knew that the Institute was built near StifleCorp. *But an underground cave connecting them? That's weird.* And on the third tunnel, where the noise was most noticeable, was a signpost saying: 'Experimentation and Processing Unit'.

He followed the third tunnel, towards the processing unit. As he emerged, he heard the unmistakable sound of Pummelcrush's voice. The strange thing was that he sounded happy.

There were other voices too. It sounded like they were celebrating.

Milo listened closely. He could just about make out Katie's voice, but it was muffled. She sounded distressed.

He moved closer, careful to remain by the cave-side beyond the reach of the light. Now there was a large glass wall, which allowed him to see into a massive room, the size of twenty football pitches, where a group of about twenty people was gathered around Dr Pummelcrush. He knew Katie must be in there, but she was hidden from sight.

'My dear friends and colleagues ...'

A hush descended, and the small crowd looked towards Pummelcrush.

'I know this is the part you've all been waiting for,' he said.

He paused.

'Welcome to our brand-new, state-of-the-art, industrial-scale human processing unit!' He lifted his arms wide and his voice boomed across the huge space. 'After many years, I am proud to say that we are ready. Ready to change the world for the better!'

There was a polite and cautious round of applause. Milo could sense the tension in the room.

Pummelcrush adopted that charming tone he could switch on so easily. 'I stumbled upon this place many years ago one evening after a particularly gruelling day teaching. As I explored the deepest, darkest recesses of the cave, a vision appeared before my eyes: what if we could rid the world of disobedience completely? What if every single child, no matter who they were or where they were from, was a top-performing, well-behaved student?'

The audience waited.

'Isn't that our goal as teachers? Isn't that what we have been striving towards for centuries? Yet no-one, until me, has had the genius to make it happen. Throughout history teachers have struggled with discipline. We just can't do our job because little brats like this one keep getting in our way. Please, close your eyes; imagine this new world. All that time wasting, all that frustration, all that punishment – gone! What would it do for our schools, our economy, our society? My dream is about to become a reality. Are you ready to join me in creating a new world?'

The crowd looked on in fear, awe and adoration. A slow, steady clap began and rose to an intense cheer.

'He truly is a genius!' Milo heard a man say.

'How exactly do you hope to pull this off?' asked a woman.

'Let me first acknowledge our partners, StifleCorp. They provide funding and technology to make our school the very best. We give them direct access to our graduates, who, after being disciplined and shaped during our six-year programme, are known to be the most loyal workers around.'

'It's true,' said a husky-voiced woman Milo recognised as Professor Borlington. 'It's been a very useful partnership. We're now the largest, most powerful tech company in the world.'

'And we are on the cusp of becoming the richest and most successful school in the world,' added Pummelcrush.

As Milo listened closely, he looked up to a sign on the cave wall that had the school's name with each word on its own line:

Secondary
Training
Institute
For
Lifelong
Employment

And it finally dawned on him. He couldn't believe his eyes: the first letter of each word in the name of the school spelled STIFLE. This partnership was no accident – it had been designed this way from the start.

'The system is perfect efficiency. We get paid by gullible parents to teach their students. We educate them to ace the SLAMs – which makes them docile, passive and obedient – and then sell them to StifleCorp.'

Sell them! Milo almost gasped out loud.

'But it takes too long,' added Borlington. 'To transform an energetic, curious child into an obedient drone takes years of daily and hourly grinding and discipline. This puts a limit on our expansion plans.'

'The key to appreciating this new world,' said Pummelcrush, 'is to see education for what it really is – a form of benevolent brainwashing.'

Scattered gasps spread across the room.

'Don't act so surprised. Am I not correct? Are they not, at root, the same thing? When we educate, do we not "reform thought"? Do we not isolate children from their environments, instil new beliefs through repetition, reward obedience and punish disobedience? Do we not demand loyalty to our institutions? All of which are the hallmarks of brainwashing.'

The crowd looked uneasy, but his convincing tone seemed to be working.

'War criminals and cult leaders have made brainwashing seem cruel. I want to show you that in fact it's an act of great charity and kindness. I want to return to its original meaning: to *wash the brain*. To cleanse it of the poison that causes children to disobey and question authority.'

Milo could see some people shake their heads. *Could these people think he has gone too far?* thought Milo. Maybe he wouldn't have to do anything. Maybe *they* would stop Pummelcrush.

But that wasn't the reaction he was hearing.

'He's right,' said one voice.

'I never thought of it like that. Yes: benevolent brainwashing!'

Praise filtered across the crowd.

Then a Disciplod spoke. 'The machine is ready, sir.'

'Is she fully and securely strapped in?'

'Yes, sir.'

'Ladies and gentlemen, I give you our latest creation: the REDUCON 6000!' Pummelcrush pulled back a grey cloth to unveil a strange-looking device suspended from the ceiling.

'The Re-Education Contraption, or REDUCON 6000, is a device that brainwashes students into complete submission so that we, as educators, can get on with our job, and you as employers and political leaders can get on with yours. No more interruptions, distractions and frustrations from independent-thinking subjects.'

'Amazing!'

'You've really done it!'

Milo didn't know what exactly he was looking at. The REDUCON 6000 was huge. It hovered over them all like a laser gun at the bottom of a brand-new fighter jet. It ran along tracks that spread across the ceiling, allowing it to move around the room. It had a massive shiny white mechanical arm. Below, a Disciplod controlled the REDUCON with simple touches of his smart-watch. The machine moved with incredible speed and pin-point precision. It swivelled and dipped as gracefully as a ballerina.

After it performed its acrobatic routine, it settled. The crowd turned to face the same direction.

Milo still couldn't quite see what they were looking at.

'The subject is a thirteen-year-old female.' Pummelcrush spoke as if reading notes.

Milo's chest tightened. He wanted to scream.

'She's in her first year,' Pummelcrush continued. 'Average grades. Misdemeanour ...' He paused to review a chart. 'She was found wandering the corridors after hours. Can you believe these spoiled little brats?'

Someone, please let her go, Milo thought.

There were tuts of disgust and disapproval.

'I didn't do anything wrong!' Katie's voice was half-muffled. 'I was heading back to the dorm.'

Milo felt like he had been hit with a hammer in the chest. *She was trying to stop me getting in trouble!*

'Shut that brat up!' Pummelcrush said, again letting his anger show. 'I said FULLY strapped in!' he yelled at the Disciplod.

'Please, no!' she pleaded.

The Disciplod barely reacted. He just walked over, his face blank, shoved a plastic mouthpiece in Katie's mouth and covered it with a strap.

Milo now got a clear look: his friend was fully restrained by thick leather straps in what appeared to be a larger, more sophisticated smart-seat.

'That's better. Please gather round and bear witness to a new era of education.'

The smooth, powerful purring of the machine filled the room. It was like a robotic cat stalking its prey.

Milo could see and just about hear Katie's struggling intensify when she heard the noise. Then the chair suddenly shot upward, propelled by a thick hydraulic arm. The seat bent at the joints like a mechanical human, moved like a transformer, laying her small body out on a platter for the machine to approach.

For a brief moment, Milo caught a glimpse of her eyes and saw pure fear.

The purring of the machine intensified as it moved towards her. She shut her eyes tight. It seems the last defence humans have against attack is to pretend – even for a moment – that what they are afraid of doesn't exist.

'Ha, ha, you see this?' Pummelcrush said, gesturing to

her eyes. Leaning close to her he went on. 'Shutting your eyes will do you no good, my dear child. You see, the REDUCON 6000 comes with automatic eye-lid expanders, which allows the brain-altering virtual reality to do its work unimpeded. The eyes are stretched wide so the subject can be submersed in the sequence without interruption.'

'Brilliant,' spluttered one man.

'The V-RES, or virtual-reality sequence, can last as long as needed and can be repeated daily for however long it takes to fully break them. Each child is unique and requires varying levels of treatment. It all depends on their mental toughness, their suggestibility. It is repeated until such time as the child no longer has the *will*, the *energy* or the *imagination* to question anything we say.'

Cheers went up around the room.

'Before long, we will have created a population of student-workers who will do and believe whatever we say.'

'This is remarkable,' said one elderly man. 'But how exactly does it work? What are you putting these kids through?'

'V-RES is a brand-new form of virtual-reality-based brainwashing. Essentially, the subject is immersed in a sequence which they believe is real. Using traditional motivators – guilt, shame, fear, disgust – the subject is conditioned to want to please and obey their master. In this case, the master is me, but it can be adapted to any organisation. The subject is reminded that the only escape from the debilitating fear is through absolute obedience. And while in a state of extreme emotional vulnerability, they'll submit and accept what they are told.'

'It's certainly innovative,' said one woman.

Professor Borlington, noticing reticence on some of the faces, stepped forward. 'Look, really we are just accelerating what an excellent education does already. We are packing six years of discipline, obedience and punishment into short, intense bursts. It might seem harsh, but think of it like ripping off a sticking plaster. In the long run, children are far freer! Free to learn and memorise and focus on what's important in the real world – passing exams, getting a good job, being productive members of society.'

Milo felt he couldn't let this happen to Katie. He *wouldn't*.

And yet, what could he do? He knew that one thirteen-year-old couldn't overpower a room full of adults. If he burst in there, they would capture him and probably give him the treatment too.

'So, when do we start?' asked another man.

'We already have,' Pummelcrush replied and nodded to his Disciplod.

The Disciplod then led a group of young students into the room. It was the students from Milo's class who had gone missing, Paul Patrick included.

They stood, eyes forward, motionless. Slowly, the crowd approached the students to get a closer look, as if they were exhibits at a museum of the absurd.

One man peered directly into Paul Patrick's eyes, and waved his plump hand back and forth. But Paul Patrick didn't flinch.

'Remarkable,' whispered the man. 'It's like I can see directly into their soul and there's nothing there.'

'Get me a drink,' he snarled at them.

But they didn't budge.

'I thought they were supposed to be obedient? Maybe he needs a top-up?'

'They are obedient,' replied Pummelcrush, 'but they don't respond to just anyone. That would be useless. You, number one, get this man a drink.'

'Yes, sir,' Paul Patrick said, and darted off to find a drink.

Pummelcrush shouted orders in quick succession: roll on the floor, jump up and down, act like a horse. And without hesitation, they did as they were told.

The room erupted in laughter. It was horrible.

'We have made the executive decision to begin the treatment of every student in the school. With the REDUCON at maximum capacity, we hope to process more students than ever before. It should be completed before graduation in May.'

'Marvellous!' cried one of the women.

'For now, our teachers are under strict instructions to find offences that need punishment so we can justify the treatment.'

'What if a child complains to their parents about being punished for little or no reason?'

'Their parents are so desperate to get their child into the school that they'll believe anything we say,' replied Pummelcrush. 'We manage the parents just as well as the kids. They might as well be brainwashed too.'

'And then we dangle an impressive-sounding career at StifleCorp in front of them and they go along with anything,' said Borlington.

'Impressive work, Finnegus. But what are the numbers?' a woman asked.

'The numbers speak for themselves. Re-education success rate of ninety-seven per cent. We found that the longer the students have been exposed to our school, the easier they are to brainwash. Strong-minded children take the longest to break. You know the ones – lots of questions, wild imaginations, the creative types. Especially in younger students – still very open-minded and not as exposed to the system. But it's only a matter of time until we find the right mix to break them also.'

'Where can I sign up?' a man at the back asked.

'Me too!'

'I need to call our director – we are going to want to go ahead straight away,' said another man.

Suddenly the whole room was bustling with orders.

Milo could see Pummelcrush, Borlington and Gurney smile.

'Please see Agnes to place orders. Remember we can set up an Institute in your local area, complete with its own REDUCON 6000, within a matter of months.'

And then, with a flick of his wrist, he gave the order: 'Begin the treatment.'

Milo desperately wanted to help Katie, but charging into the room would be totally useless.

The arm moved slowly, deliberately, towards Katie. It made contact with her eyes, which were prised open by the two metal prongs, each with circular rubber pads at the end. A virtual-reality headset slid down to cover the top half of her face, like a pair of bug-eyed sunglasses.

They all stood around and watched.

Every so often her body would twitch, recoil and spasm.

There were nods of approval, but after a while they began turning away and chatting.

'Let's leave the machine to do its work. We will send you some sample sequences: they are frightening even for adults. Let's go upstairs and sign some contracts. Perhaps another drink to celebrate?'

Everyone started leaving the room.

Milo crouched behind some crates so as not to be seen as they came out into the corridor. If they all left now, he could rescue Katie without being noticed. But then he saw Pummelcrush look up and down the corridor, take out his keys and lock the door.

No! Milo said to himself. He watched as Pummelcrush checked to make sure the door was locked and then followed the others towards the lift.

As soon as the corridor was empty, Milo bolted for the door Pummelcrush had locked, though he knew it was probably pointless. He grabbed the handle. He pushed, pulled, yanked and jiggled it. He shouted and banged the door. It was no good.

It was getting late now, and soon Milo would have to be in bed or the sensors would alert Du-Ped that he was missing. He had to make the agonising decision to leave his best friend behind the locked door, in the clutches of that terrible machine. It broke his heart.

He promised himself that no matter what happened, he would do everything he could to bring Katie back from wherever she was going now.

There must be a way, he thought as he went back to his room. And then it hit him: *That's it!*

That thing that Pummelcrush had said — that strong-minded kids, the ones who ask questions, who are curious, who think for themselves, they are tough to break. That was it. The philosophy Milo and his friends had been practising with Ursula! It was certainly making them ask questions and think for themselves. And if that meant they would be tough to break, maybe it could also work the other way around. Maybe it could help to bring Katie back to herself after the treatment?

Chapter 10

Anybody can become angry, that is easy;
but to be angry with the right person,
and to the right degree, and at the right time,
for the right purpose, and in the right way,
that is not within everybody's power and is not easy.
— Aristotle

Pummelcrush came into class the following morning, blowing his big drippy nose in a white handkerchief. It sounded like an elephant playing the trumpet. When he finished blowing, he unfolded the sopping handkerchief, looked inside it and made a face. He then tossed it over his head and barked, 'Hold on to this for the day and wash it for me later.'

Milo and Sarah-Louise looked at each other. They would hate to have to carry around Pummelcrush's dirty handkerchief. Then their faces dropped: the student who was following Pummelcrush, carefully putting the soggy handkerchief away, was Katie. Her expression was blank, her eyes were dull. You could hear the squelch as she put the hanky into her pocket. There was no way the real Katie would do something like that. *She's gone,* thought Milo.

He watched her walk towards her seat, waiting for her to look up and greet her friends like she always did. But Katie just walked, robot-like, behind Pummelcrush and waited at his side. He waved her off, and she headed for her seat without looking up.

'Now, I hope you have all noticed how well-behaved some of our students have been lately. Isn't that right, Katie?'

'Yes, Dr Pummelcrush. The Secondary Training Institute for Lifelong Employment is an elite school. We are honoured to be here.' She spoke with no expression. All the music in her voice, the breezy lilt and cadence of it, was gone, replaced with a dull flatness.

'That's right. Why can't the rest of you behave like her? Watch how she focuses and keeps quiet.'

Pummelcrush stared off for a moment, then came back to finish his thought: 'But don't worry, you will all find out soon.'

Milo was the only one who really knew what he meant by that.

'What is wrong with Katie?' Sarah-Louise asked Milo after class.

Milo told her everything.

'You were right, Milo,' said Sarah-Louise, horrified at what Milo had just told her. 'I should have believed you. What can we do?'

'I don't know,' said Milo. 'But let's see what Ursula thinks. She might be able to help.'

* * *

'Where's Katie?' Ursula asked, when Milo and Sarah-Louise arrived into her garden that evening.

'We lost her,' said Milo, getting visibly upset. 'She has become one of *them*.'

'Now, now, calm down – just tell me what happened,' said Ursula.

'I know what the treatment is now. I saw Katie get it,' said Milo.

'We both saw Katie this morning in class,' added Sarah-Louise. 'She's been turned into a brain-dead zombie-robot, just like the Disciplods.'

'The school has been brainwashing the students for years,' said Milo, 'but now they have a machine that does it way faster, turns the students into human robots. And they are then *selling* them to StifleCorp and other places as slave workers. I heard them *gloating* about it.'

'I knew they were up to *something*,' said Ursula, shocked. 'But *this* …'

'They are planning to brainwash as many kids as they can,' Milo went on, 'first in this school, then the rest of the world.'

'That's why they want the number one ranking so badly,' said Sarah-Louise. 'So they can open up branches in other countries and brainwash as many children as they can.'

Ursula just sat, thinking.

'I saw the machine with my own eyes,' said Milo. 'And poor Katie, strapped to it. But, listen – there's something I heard that might help.'

'What's that?' asked Ursula.

'I heard them saying that strong, questioning minds are the hardest to break. And this is especially true for younger students, who haven't been exposed to the system as long.

They have more open minds, are more questioning and their imaginations are more active.'

'Well, in that case,' said Ursula, standing up, 'we need to start training as many students as possible in philosophy, to strengthen their minds and keep them open and questioning, so they won't be so susceptible to this horrible treatment.'

'Yes!' Sarah-Louise said. 'We were thinking the same thing. We think Consuela, Liam and Gerry would be up for it.'

'Let me talk to the school authorities so I can expand my "gardening group". You two can help by recruiting more students. We will train them so that we make it as difficult as possible for them to be brainwashed.'

'Yes,' said Milo, 'but we also need to find a way to stop what Pummelcrush and his gang are doing. It will be the Christmas holidays soon, and that will be our chance to talk to our parents without the school spying on us.'

'Good idea, Milo.'

Milo and Sarah-Louise left the garden feeling a bit better. Their hearts were broken about Katie, but they had a plan, and that gave them hope – and sometimes that is all you need to keep going.

Chapter 11

*The highest education is that which
does not merely give us information
but makes our life in harmony with all existence.*
– Rabindranath Tagore

Exam week came around fast. Everyone had moved into study overdrive. These exams were the last the sixth-years would sit before they would begin the final preparation for the defining moment of their lives, and the school: the SLAMs. The anxiety and panic that usually marked the atmosphere around the Institute had risen to a state of vibrating frenzy. Corridors were lined with huddled groups of hysterical students obsessively revising.

For the first-years, these exams determined their final ranking in the class. The results were publicly displayed on screens around the school. Also, they would be the key feature of the school reports. Du-Ped corrected exams as they were being written. Results would be revealed to parents straight away.

The week passed in a blur. Milo and Sarah-Louise were kept so busy by study and school duties that they didn't get a chance to approach their classmates about their plan before the end of term and the Christmas holidays.

Milo was relieved to be home, but it took him some time to adjust to the freedom to do whatever he wanted – within reason. The best thing was being able to eat decent food again: crisps, chocolate, popcorn, sausages and chips – all his favourites.

One night, as he and his parents sat in the kitchen eating dinner, his dad asked, 'Milo, is everything OK with you? You seem quiet.'

'Well, not really,' he replied, cautiously at first.

'You can talk to us, Milo,' said his mam. 'What's wrong?'

Milo looked up and saw in his parents' eyes that they cared about him.

'Well –' He paused and took a breath. This was his chance to tell them what had been going on at the Institute. 'I hate that school! I hate everything about it. And I found out that they have been brainwashing students using a machine and are selling them to StifleCorp as slave-workers. They plan to brainwash as many kids as they can.'

Milo looked up slowly, expecting his parents to be shocked. But when he met their eyes, they were smiling. Not a happy smile, but a pitying, patronising smile. They glanced at each other and nodded.

'Why are you looking at me like that?' asked Milo.

'Milo, it's fine. We know everything.' His dad spoke in a tone that could only be described as condescending.

'What do you mean, you know everything?'

'It's OK, Milo,' his mam said. She reached across the table and placed her hand on his. 'We are not mad at you.'

'Mad at me? Why would you be mad at me?'

'Look, Milo …' His dad hesitated for a moment. 'We know you have been getting in a bit of trouble. We know you have been struggling to adapt to the system. We get the updates. But that's OK with us. We understand it takes time.'

'Yes, honey, we've spoken to the school counsellor a number of times,' his mam said proudly. 'She is such an impressive and caring woman'.

'We've become quite friendly with Agnes,' said his dad.

'Agnes? You mean Mrs Gurney? Caring? Are you crazy?' Milo said, utterly bamboozled by what he was hearing.

'Yes, Mrs Gurney. And Dr Pummelcrush, many times.' His dad shook his head. 'I'm still amazed that a man of his stature takes the time to contact the parents directly.'

'Wait – are we talking about the same people? They are the cruellest people I ever met. They're turning us into zombies!'

Milo's dad smiled again and turned to his mam. 'This is almost exactly what Finnegus said he would say. Remarkable.'

'Milo, this is perfectly normal for first-years. It's a big change. It's a famous institution with their own way of doing things. You just have to buckle down.'

'Mam? Do you buy this too? You don't believe what I'm telling you?'

'Of course I believe you, Milo, my love. It's just that – well, when you think the teachers are being unfair, they are really doing what's best for you. They are working at the best school in the country. Sure, it's tough, but once you get used to it, it will stand to you in the long run.'

They even used Pummelcrush's phrases.

'No, look, you don't understand. I know you THINK you know what's going on. But it's waaaaaay worse! I've seen their secret lab, underneath in the caves, the brainwashing machine. I've seen kids change, even Katie! They are destroying us.'

His dad let out a small laugh. 'Milo, seriously, you don't expect us to actually believe this, do you? How could the best school in Ireland hide a secret brainwashing lab? And I spoke to Katie's parents. She is recovering from a virus so she might not be herself for a while, that's all.'

'That's a lie!' said Milo. 'Please, you have to believe me.'

'THAT'S ENOUGH!' His dad had suddenly flipped. He banged his fist on the table, making Milo jump.

'You need to grow up,' his dad yelled. 'I'm sorry, but the world is a tough place. Do you have any idea what we sacrificed to get you into this school? Bloody hell, the amount of overtime we've worked ...'

Milo's mam placed a hand on her husband's arm to try and calm him down.

'OK, Max, calm down, please.'

Milo's dad took a deep breath. 'Look, we want what's best for you, Milo. Please, just accept this is what you have to do. You'll thank us in the long run.'

'Your dad doesn't mean to be angry,' Milo's mam said in a soothing tone. 'You need to really focus, Milo. We know you can do it. Now, who'd like some dessert?' she asked, as she got up from the table and began clearing away the plates, the sign that the conversation was over.

Milo was speechless, flabbergasted. Pummelcrush, that sneaky operator, had gotten to his parents before he could.

He was good, thought Milo, shaking his head, he was very good.

They finished their dessert in silence.

Once again he felt small, powerless and voiceless. Once again he was dealing with adults who wouldn't listen, hear him or believe him. He was angry but he didn't want to ruin Christmas. He knew his parents were wrong, but he also knew that if he wanted to help Katie, he had to act like everything was fine – for now.

As the holidays wore on, Milo could see his parents were really trying to make this Christmas special. He tried hard to hang on to this sense of gratitude for the rest of the holiday, but the anger at not being believed was always there. How can a person feel both gratitude and anger towards the same people?

He knew now that it was up to him to stop Pummelcrush and expose the school. Up to him and Sarah-Louise and Ursula – and whoever else they could get on board.

Chapter 12

*It is a narrow mind which cannot look
at a subject from various points of view.*
– George Eliot

The first day back at the Institute was a celebration. Another chance for the school to enhance its own mythical status. The occasion was centred around Pummelcrush's message for the new year. With Gurney whispering in his ear, he strode onto the stage. All the other teachers stood meekly in the background, faces hidden in the shadows and heads hung down.

'Welcome back, students!' Pummelcrush spoke faster than usual, his voice a couple of tones higher, more frantic. 'This is no ordinary semester. No, no, no,' he repeated as he paced. 'This is the most special semester in the school's entire history. This is the year that we can take our place as the number one school in the entire world.'

His hands shot up in the air as the sixth-years cheered. Milo rolled his eyes; he now knew their vigorous support was only a product of years of brainwashing. He pitied them.

'However, we are not there yet,' Pummelcrush continued. 'Everything must go according to plan.' His voice was getting louder. 'That means I will tolerate nothing less than utter obedience. Complete surrender. Complete devotion to me and the Institute.'

He took long strides in his brand-new pinstriped suit. He wiped beads of sweat off his reddened forehead with a clenched fist of white knuckles. 'That means no asking questions, no talking back, no messing, no complaining, no pretending to be sick, no weakness at all. I warn you!'

Milo could see the pressure was getting to Pummelcrush. He seemed deranged.

Gurney whispered in his ear. He stopped pacing, calmed himself and stood still.

'My dear students, we need to show the world that this truly is the best school. Throughout the year you will see inspectors and distinguished visitors checking the school. All you need to do – all you ever need to do – is put your head down and shut up.'

The Disciplods began shouting: 'Number one! Number one!' Until the whole school was in a frenzy, chanting along with them. Milo and Sarah-Louise looked at Katie, who was chanting passionately.

It made Milo sad, but also determined. He looked at the other first-year students. They joined in the chanting, but without the same crazed intensity as the older students. Milo knew that the first-years were the only hope to prevent Pummelcrush's plans. *It's up to us to resist*, he thought. *We are the only ones who can stop this.*

Back in class, Pummelcrush was supercharged. The pace at which they went through the lesson plans – maths, business, computer science, accounting – increased.

Plus, they really had to watch their facial expressions even more carefully now. Over the break, more top-of-the-range HD cameras had been installed at every corner. Every single facial expression, no matter how slight, would be recorded, added to your file and followed by a punishment.

After a few days of the repetitive routine, Milo felt anxious and impatient. They had to recruit the group without being detected.

The Disciplods, while still on patrol, had begun to focus on their number one priority: preparing for the SLAMs. Motivational slogans were everywhere:

Good luck to our warriors as they ready for battle!
Do not dare let us down!

The only thing that kept Milo focused was the thought of creating a resistance against Pummelcrush. So, when the weekend came, Sarah-Louise and Milo didn't waste any time before approaching some of their classmates.

They talked to Consuela Petherbridge first.

'Psssst,' Milo leaned in to her ear, while looking straight ahead.

'Yeah, pssst,' Sarah-Louise echoed into the other ear.

'Eh? Are you pssting at me?' Consuela asked.

'Yeah, we are. Do you want to join a secret philosophy resistance squad?'

'A *what*?' asked Consuela. 'Resisting what?'

'You've noticed what happened to Katie, Paul Patrick and the others?' asked Milo.

'Of course,' Consuela answered, checking to see no-one else heard. 'What's Pummelcrush done to them?'

'They've been brainwashed,' said Sarah-Louise. 'And we could be next. But we might have a way to protect ourselves.'

'What?' Consuela said, her eyes darting around nervously. 'We shouldn't even be talking about this, not here.'

'Look, trust us,' said Milo. 'If you want to avoid becoming a slave for the rest of your life, then meet us on Corridor 2B on Friday evening after dinner.'

Milo pulled out a piece of paper with the details: *Friday, 6pm, Corridor 2B.*

'Just be there!' he said, pressing the piece of paper on Consuela.

Milo and Sarah-Louise started looking around, scoping out their next potential recruit.

'What about him?' asked Milo, pointing to a boy at the next table who was feeding himself spoonfuls of paste.

As Milo watched, he saw him miss his mouth several times, the paste dripping down his chin.

'Hmm, I dunno. Think he might be too far gone already,' said Sarah-Louise.

'Well, what about Julia Conlon?' suggested Milo.

'Miss Perfect? Are you mad?'

Milo knew that Sarah-Louise was still upset that Julia beat her in the class rankings several times last term.

'Yes, Miss Perfect. She knows something is amiss. Pummelcrush would never suspect her of anything either.'

'Eugh, OK, fine.'

Over the next few days, they managed to talk to several other first-year students.

On Friday evening, Sarah-Louise stood outside the grey door on Corridor 2B and waited for people to arrive. Milo was positioned a little further down the hall around the corner to keep an eye out in case he had to explain to any Disciplods that they were the gardening volunteers.

Before long, he spotted Consuela.

'Psst,' Milo said as he pointed her to Sarah-Louise. 'Remember, we are gardening volunteers.'

And then Liam and Gerry Burke walked towards him.

'Quickly, look, straight down there,' Milo whispered.

'On the ball, Milo, boy, no bother,' they said together.

Before long, all the students they had invited showed up. As they entered the garden, they were met with a wonderful smell. Milo closed his eyes for a second to breathe it in. Then he saw Ursula and a table laid out with delicious food.

There was a feast: freshly baked scones, slices of apple coated in peanut butter and drizzled with the school's own honey, salted crackers with slices of crumbly cheddar cheese and a big bowl of juicy red grapes. And there was a large teapot, wisps of steam floating out of its spout.

'Wow!' said Consuela. 'What is this place?' She and the others moved from the table to the flowers and hanging baskets.

'This is such a cute little garden!' said Julia.

'It's class!' said Liam.

'So many colours! Wait, what are you doing here, Julia?' asked Gerry, surprised to see the top student disobeying the school.

'Yes, I know, surprise, surprise. But I'm as concerned as you are,' Julia said.

'Welcome!' said Ursula. 'My name is Ursula. I'm the school gardener, but I used to teach here. I'm so glad you could all make it. Let's gather round. There is no time to spare.'

As she said this, Milo was stuffing an entire scone slathered with butter and strawberry jam into his mouth.

'Please, everyone, take a seat,' said Ursula.

The students all sat around her, wearing their winter coats, on the small stools and mini bean bags that she had put out for them. There were blankets too, and extra cushions.

'Now, I thought it might be nice to remind you what real food is like,' Ursula said, passing around the plates of delicious treats. 'Please help yourselves. And while you do, Milo is going to say a few words about what is going on here.'

'Excuse me,' Milo said, rushing to swallow and clear his throat as crumbs fell from his lips. 'Thanks for coming. The reason you're here is because there is something very bad happening. We've discovered that the school has been torturing and brainwashing kids in order to make them into ultra-obedient students, and then selling them as slave-workers to StifleCorp.'

'What? Are you serious?'

'That can't be true!'

'How do you know for sure?'

'We need to tell our parents.'

'Please, everyone, listen!' said Sarah-Louise, standing up. 'It's true. Our best friend Katie has been completely brainwashed. So much that she is no longer the same lovely person. You've seen Paul Patrick and the others. Milo saw it happen with his own eyes ...' She trailed off, upset. 'Tell them, Milo.'

'It's true – I followed them when they caught Katie. They brought her to a huge cave underneath the school. There is a tunnel connecting to StifleCorp. They've a special machine, called the REDUCON 6000, which brainwashes kids until they accept what they are told without question.'

'But why?'

'Because Pummelcrush wants to create a world of obedient controllable children and become crazy rich while he is at it.'

'Is this true?' Consuela asked Ursula.

'I'm afraid so. I've long suspected there was something bad happening here. But I had no idea it was this bad.'

'So, what do we do?' asked Liam. 'We should tell our parents, right?'

Milo and Ursula looked at each other. 'I'm afraid we can't tell our parents just yet,' Milo said. 'Part of the Institute's strategy is to kind of brainwash the parents before they even start on the students. They have the parents so convinced it's the perfect school that they are willing to ignore any complaints from their children.'

'I know! My parents wouldn't believe me. Any time I've complained – they just tell me to get on with it,' said Consuela. 'If I told them this now they would think I'm just exaggerating to get their attention.'

'Ahhh me too,' said Julia. 'My grandmother thinks children should be seen and not heard. Nobody listens to us.'

'Exactly,' said Sarah-Louise. 'Same here.'

'So – what, then?' asked Gerry looking at his twin brother, who was nodding in agreement. 'How can we stop them ourselves?'

'There is one small piece of hope,' said Milo, looking at Ursula.

'We know,' said Ursula, 'that the brainwashing machine has one weakness: children with strong, open, questioning minds cannot be brainwashed so easily. The machine works best on those who are already susceptible to believing whatever they are told.'

'Right,' said Milo, 'so the first thing we need to do is to train our minds to be more open, questioning and strong. And we do that by practising philosophy.'

'Philosophy?' said Julia.

'What's philosophy?' Consuela asked.

Ursula smiled and launched into her explanation of philosophy.

She told them how it begins in wonder, wonder at the very fact of existence. Wonder that we are here in the world, in the universe, and we don't know why or where we came from. She told them how it's about trying to understand what it means to be a human in the world, who are we and what should we do? She told them how it seeks to explore the parts of reality we don't fully understand. How it asks questions that don't have simple and clear answers. Can we know what reality is really like? Or do we only know how it appears to us? Is the world fair? Or do the powerful always get their way? Are people fully responsible for their actions? Or are they just the result of their upbringing?

The students sat trying to take everything in.

'But most of all,' Ursula continued, 'practising philosophy helps you develop a questioning and open mind. It helps you to be comfortable in uncertainty and doubt. Life and the world are a mystery and we need to face that mystery together, and not retreat into simple beliefs just because it feels safer. Philosophy can help us do that.'

'I'm not sure I understand,' said Liam.

'I didn't either, at the start,' said Milo. 'But the more I practised it, the more I saw what it was.'

'So how do we practise it?' asked Consuela.

'Through conversation,' replied Ursula, as Milo poured out mugs of tea for everyone. 'You see, some really important questions about life are very complicated and difficult, and after thousands of years of trying to answer them, we still don't know! Did the universe have a beginning? Is it fair that some people have more than others? What's the difference between courage and stupidity? Because these questions are tricky to answer, the best way to do it is together, with other people, hearing other views and ideas. And that is philosophy.'

Milo saw the other students nodding. He smiled at Ursula. He knew it was her kindness and her energy that had got them on board.

URSULA: Now, first, I want everyone to take a deep breath, close your eyes, and bring your mind into the present moment, into your body. Remember, this is very important if you want to do philosophy with other people. You must be fully present. You must listen to each other and really hear what people have to say. I can't tell you how many times in conversations people don't really listen, but only wait for their chance to talk.

Milo and the others took a deep breath and brought their focus to the present moment.

URSULA: So, here is a thought-experiment.

CONSUELA: A thought-experiment? What's that?

URSULA: It's like a 'what-if' game. It's a way of imagining a situation and then exploring what it be might like if that was true.

CONSUELA: Oh, OK, cool.

URSULA: So, imagine I had a special crystal bottle of liquid, shiny blue and glowing, and if you drank it, you would have everlasting life: would you drink it?

JULIA: A drink that made you immortal?

URSULA: Yes. No death. No dying. You would live for ever.

MILO: Yes, obviously. Duh. Wouldn't everyone? That's like the most classic wish people have!

URSULA: I wouldn't.

LIAM: What? Are you serious? Aren't you afraid of dying, though?

URSULA: Of course I am. But that doesn't mean I would choose to avoid it.

MILO: But, if you could live for ever, think of all the extra stuff you could do.

URSULA: I know – there are so many things I would love to do. But think about it, Milo: it's FOR EVVERRR!

Ursula put on a scary voice and made claws of her hands.

MILO (laughing): I know. I get it.

URSULA: Yes, but I'm not sure you appreciate what it really means. For ever is not just living to a hundred, or a thousand, or a billion … it's FOR EVER. For the rest of eternity. That's an incomprehensible amount of time.

CONSUELA: Oh! For ever is *long*. But still, think of all the things I could do!

GERRY: Wait! How old would you be? Would you be healthy? Rich? Like, if I stayed my age now, I'd be too young.

URSULA: Very good clarifying questions, young man. What age would you like to be?

GERRY: Hmm, I dunno, twenty-seven? That seems old enough to be taken seriously, but young enough to have a good time.

URSULA: Fine. You can be twenty-seven, healthy and have enough money so you don't have to worry about it, but not too much.

GERRY: OK, great. Bring it on! I have so much to do.

URSULA: You are saying the reason you'd want to live for ever is to have more time to do more things?

GERRY: Yeah, well, to experience more of life and the world. That's my dream.

URSULA: Like what?

GERRY: I could master every sport, maybe even turn pro: soccer, basketball, rugby.

LIAM: Don't forget hurling, football, tennis, all of them!

MILO: And I could learn all the musical instruments, become a jazz trumpeter, a rock and roll drummer and a blues piano player.

SARAH-LOUISE: Oh, I'd get to play and complete all my favourite video games.

JULIA: I'd like to travel the world and climb all the biggest mountains and swim in far-off seas and lakes. Imagine! Getting to see all the animals, elephants, tigers, lions …

URSULA: Don't forget dogs! I love dogs.

JULIA: Yeah, me too. But we see dogs all the time.

URSULA: True. What else would you do?

SARAH-LOUISE: It would be cool to see what kind of technologies get made in the future … like time travel or something to make us invisible.

URSULA: Oh, yes, it would be quite interesting to see what inventions we would develop.

MILO: And then all the new movies, music and everything. It would be so much fun. And think of the people you could help, with all the knowledge and experience you'd have after thousands of years. You could use your wisdom to help others.

Milo's eyes were bright and wide. He was alive when he was using his imagination.

URSULA: You make a good case, everyone. I bet living for ever with you would be really fun.

MILO: Actually ... could you have a partner, or a buddy? Someone to live for ever with you?

URSULA: No, I'm afraid not, Milo. For this thought-experiment you'd be the only one with eternal life.

This caused the group to stop for a moment and think. Milo's imagination wandered. He found himself being propelled into the future at great speed. He watched as civilisations rose and fell in front of his eyes. But he also saw himself loving and losing friends and family, time and time again.

MILO: Hmm ...

URSULA: What's wrong?

MILO: Well, I suppose that if I was to live for ever then I'd outlast my grandparents, my parents, my friends and everyone I know. Everyone who is on earth right now and everyone who is ever going to be on earth. If I had a family and kids, I'd have to watch them get older and change, and I'd stay the same. Then I'd have to watch them pass on. Eventually everyone I know or ever got to know would be gone and I'd still be here.

URSULA: And do you think that would make it too difficult?

MILO: I'm not sure. I suppose I hadn't considered how lonely and hard it would be to live for ever when no-one else did.

SARAH-LOUISE: But I could meet new people all the time? And have new families?

URSULA: Sure, of course, but remember, for ever is for ever. So you'd have to go through that loss many times, hundreds, thousands, millions, billions.

CONSUELA: Yeah – that would be tough all right. You would feel lonely.

JULIA: And perhaps bored?

GERRY: Bored? How would you be bored with all the things to do?

SARAH-LOUISE: Yeah, but after a while, think about it. You'd have done everything. And then done everything again, three times, four times. You could do things so many times, surely, eventually you'd just get so fed up and bored of doing anything. If you lived for ever, time might as well stand still.

GERRY: I don't know about that one.

URSULA: No? You think things could remain interesting and worth doing for ever?

GERRY: Well, what's something you do every day?

URSULA: I have a cup of tea every single day, usually more than one.

GERRY: And you don't get bored of that do you?

URSULA: No, I suppose not.

GERRY: But you know what tea tastes like, you know how to make it, there are no surprises. But yet you still like to do it.

URSULA: I like that thought. Making tea is almost like a sacred ritual.

LIAM: Yeah, exactly! It's like a thing that we make special because we decide it's special.

MILO: Right. It's not that the thing itself has to be entertaining or exciting. It's that we give it meaning.

JULIA: Yeah. Although, could we be strong enough to give things meaning for ever?

CONSUELA: I'm not sure.

MILO: Me neither.

URSULA: That's the beauty of philosophy. You don't have to choose. It's OK to be uncertain, to have doubts. This is a tough question.

SARAH-LOUISE: I guess we don't have to decide, because it's not likely to happen.

URSULA: Probably not – but you never know. One day in the future we could be faced with that choice.

MILO: I suppose it's possible.

URSULA: But regardless, it's not about finding out the right answer: maybe there is no right answer. It's about having the freedom to ask questions, any questions, even ones that seem silly at first.

LIAM: What do you mean, silly?

URSULA: Well, I bet Dr Pummelcrush would think it's a waste of time to have a discussion about immortality, that it's a silly question. That it has nothing to do with anything 'serious' or 'important'. But we were also discussing what makes life meaningful. And what could be more important than that?'

MILO: We were?

URSULA: Yes, of course. By doing a thought-experiment like this, where we play around with the idea of living for ever, we are also discussing its opposite: the fact that we don't live for ever. And while that might seem like a bad thing at first, as we explored it, we ended up saying that maybe it's good, maybe it's what makes life special. Maybe the shortness of life is what makes us appreciate the things we have.

SARAH-LOUISE: Ah, I think I understand. I'm not sure why, but it makes me happy to be alive.

Ursula smiled. These kids really seemed to have enjoyed their first philosophy conversation.

'Every time we have these conversations, it's like the world, the school and all other problems just melt into the background,' Milo said.

'Yeah, I felt that too,' said Sarah-Louise.

'Yes,' said Ursula. 'That happens when you fully engage in something or lose yourself in an activity. It's a wonderful state to be in. But now it's time for you guys to leave. And please, Milo and everyone, remember to be careful. We don't want any of you getting caught. Not until we figure out how to stop them. We need all of you. And we need you to keep questioning, keep thinking.'

'Thanks so much for this, Ursula,' said Liam. He took another scone from the table.

'Cheers!' said Gerry, snatching the scone from his brother just as he was about to take a bite, which made everyone laugh.

'Yeah, it was great,' said Julia, 'way better than our normal class!'

'Aw, you're very welcome,' replied Ursula.

* * *

Over the next few months the group met several more times. Since they began meeting together and talking, Milo and his friends had become stronger, mentally and emotionally. They no longer walked with slumped shoulders. Their eyes no longer fell away from Pummelcrush's stare. They had purpose. They met his eyes boldly: there was no rule against that. But he hated it.

Milo could see his eyebrow lift in suspicion when they entered class one day after a philosophy session, laughing and joking. Pummelcrush was eternally suspicious of carefree, light-hearted happiness.

He growled at them and whispered something to Katie, who had become his number one slave. As he whispered, he stared at Milo.

It took all Milo's strength not to smirk right back at him. But he knew that any slight provocation could mean he would get the treatment. He had too many responsibilities to be so careless. He needed to destroy Pummelcrush, the Institute and StifleCorp. That's all.

Students were still disappearing. Almost one a week. Milo knew that it wasn't enough for the secret philosophy resistance squad to casually meet and train their minds, as enjoyable as that was. They also needed to come up with a plan to stop brainwashing.

Chapter 13

Abundance of knowledge
does not teach men to be wise.
— Heraclitus

The philosophy resistance squad met again just before the school's big graduation celebration. They gathered under the tree in Ursula's garden and brought themselves into the present moment.

URSULA: The purpose of life is to be happy. Now, who agrees with that?'

CONSUELA: I agree!

URSULA: Why?

CONSUELA: Well, because happiness is the best feeling we have — when you are happy, you don't want anything to change. You want whatever is making you happy to stay. I just think everything we do is in order to be happy.

JULIA: You think so? I'm not so sure.

CONSUELA: Yes, of course — when we watch a movie, hang out with our friends, listen to music, that's all to make us happy. Everyone always talks about happiness as being the best thing.

JULIA: Fair enough, but what about when we cry at a sad movie or song? Or help a friend who is feeling down. You don't do those things to make you happy, do you?

CONSUELA: Hmm, good point. Well, maybe you do – in the long run, maybe feeling sad for a moment or being there for a friend is what makes you happy.

MILO: Yeah, I was going to say something similar. I think there is a difference between pleasure and happiness.

LIAM: What's the difference? Aren't they just two words for the same thing?

MILO: I don't think so. Pleasure is something that just happens for a moment. And happiness is something more long-lasting. Like you can be a happy person generally.

SARAH-LOUISE: Maybe – but either way, I don't think it's possible to be happy all the time.

CONSUELA: It might not be possible, but the question was about the purpose of life. It's the aim – what we are striving for, right?

GERRY: I don't know if it's a good purpose even – to try and be happy all the time. It sounds like a lot of pressure. Then when you're not happy, you might think you're doing something wrong, or failing. You know?

JULIA: Yeah, I agree. I kind of think that you can only be happy if sometimes you are sad, or angry, or frustrated. It's OK to feel those emotions too.

CONSUELA: I'm not disagreeing that we will face other emotions, but I still think that the best time in life is when we are happy, and that we should try and be happy as much as possible.

URSULA: I have another thought-experiment. Imagine the REDUCON, but instead of brainwashing you to be dumb and obedient, it made you believe you were living the perfect life – everything you ever wanted, dreamed of and desired could be yours. But it wouldn't be real – in reality, your real body would be just sitting motionless in a chair all day and all night, for all time. But you would see, hear and feel everything as real. Would you choose to hook up?

CONSUELA: Yes, that would be amazing.

MILO: No way!

URSULA: Why not? You could have everything you ever wanted.

MILO: Well, because it's not real. It's fake, or pretend.

CONSUELA: Why does that matter?

MILO: I'm not quite sure, but it just seems weird to me to live in a fake fantasy land. What's the point in living? It's not a challenge any more.

JULIA: I agree with Milo. Life is a challenge for sure, but that's what makes it interesting. If you just quit and go and hide out in a pleasure cave, then you're not really living.

LIAM: Yeah, same, but for me it's because you're not connecting with anything or anyone. You're not connecting with the rest of the world. The happiness we have been talking about is all about the individual. It's kind of selfish. I think life is about how we connect and relate to others and the world around us.

URSULA: Oh, that's interesting. I like that idea.

Liam smiled, proud of his comment.

CONSUELA: I like that idea too, but I still think the purpose is to be happy. A good way to be happy is through connection with others and the world.

MILO: Who says there is a purpose to life anyway? Why does there have to be?

LIAM: Yeah, Ursula, what do you mean by 'purpose'?

URSULA: You tell me what you think it means.

LIAM: I suppose to have a purpose is to have a goal, or aim, or a meaning. It's like the reason why we do things, the reason why we get up in the morning and keep going?

URSULA: That sounds about right. So do you think life has a purpose?

SARAH-LOUISE: I would say it's just to procreate, to continue on with the species, same as any other living thing.

GERRY: Who says that is the purpose?

SARAH-LOUISE: No-one says it, but at the end of the day, that is what all living things strive for – to find ways to keep their species going.

JULIA: Does that mean people who choose not to

have children have failed at the purpose of life? Don't think I like the sound of that!

SARAH-LOUISE: That seems a bit harsh all right.

MILO: I think we create our own purpose. You can choose what your purpose is, and it can change, but it's up to you to decide rather than find out or be told.

URSULA: I like that thought too. And I think doing philosophy can help you figure that out.

As the group went on talking, they suddenly noticed a series of drone-balls shooting down from the sky at great speed. For a moment, they thought they were under attack. As they reached the garden, the eight drone-balls stopped dead and hovered over their heads in a perfect circle, silent, but shining a spotlight on each person. And just as they got up to investigate, BANG! The door burst open.

The hum of lively conversation stopped dead as the students and Ursula turned in shock.

Dr Pummelcrush was standing at the door, his face contorted in fury and disbelief. And by his side, expression-less, were Katie and Paul Patrick, with four Disciplods right behind, their dull-eyed stare made all the more frightening by pure exhaustion.

'WHAT IS THE MEANING OF THIS?' yelled Pummelcrush.

'Finnegus, calm down,' said Ursula, moving into position between him and the kids. 'There's nothing to worry about, this is just our gardening group.'

'Don't give me that nonsense! I know full well there are no vegetables growing here.'

'Finnegus, please, take it easy,' said Ursula.

'Don't you dare challenge me, woman,' he shouted, pulling back his fist as if he was going to throw a punch at Ursula. 'You pathetic pitiful excuse for a teacher. Gardening, my eye. I should have cast you out of here when I had the chance!'

'Hey, don't speak to her like that,' said Milo, moving towards Pummelcrush.

Ursula held him back as the Disciplods took a step forward and grabbed Milo by the arms to protect their master. Pummelcrush jumped back, unused to being confronted. He regained his composure, safe behind his adolescent bodyguards.

'Don't hurt him!' said Ursula.

'Shut it,' said Pummelcrush to Ursula. He turned to face Milo, who was struggling in the Disciplods' tight grasp.

'And you!' Pummelcrush screamed at Milo, shaking with frenzied anger. 'I should have known you'd have something to do with this. I demand to know exactly what is going on here.'

Ursula mouthed to everyone: 'Everything will be OK.'

'It's nothing to worry about, Finnegus,' she said, employing the most soothing tone she could muster. 'A couple of students just dropped by to chat, that's all.'

'We don't have time for chatting here. Chatting about what? I don't believe that for a minute. What are you plotting? What do you know?'

'Take it easy,' said Ursula, moving a step closer, as if taming a wild animal. 'We just chat about life and the universe and everything in between! Isn't that right?'

'Yeah, it's nothing bad,' said Sarah-Louise. It was the first time she had ever spoken up against him. She looked over at Julia and nodded.

'Dr Pummelcrush, we just talk about the meaning of life and things like that,' said Julia defiantly.

Everyone gasped. Here was Pummelcrush's favourite student standing up to him.

'This is an outrage,' he shouted. 'Students sneaking off. Never in all my years have I witnessed such insubordination!' He was pacing now. 'And to think –' He stopped in front of Ursula. 'After everything, after I graciously allowed you to stay on here, you stab me in the back. Such nonsense!'

'It's not nonsense. The students have a lot of questions they don't get to ask in school, they have a lot of things to say, so they talk here.'

'Don't give me that blather again. If we had listened to you and your philosophy mumbo-jumbo, do you think we'd be on the cusp of being named the best school in the world?'

Pummelcrush kicked over a pot of purple flowers, stamping on the fragile petals.

'All of you,' he said, pointing to the students, 'I'm bringing you for processing right this instant. I'll make sure you NEVER disobey me again! Take them down below!'

The Disciplods clicked their watches, freezing everyone's uniforms. They began grabbing the students and yanking them out of the garden.

Ursula protested. 'Finnegus, don't do this. I'm sorry. It's all my fault. We will stop the meetings. Just don't do it to them.'

He turned sharply. 'Don't do what? What do you know?' he asked, peering at her through his narrow green eyes.

'I don't know anything,' said Ursula. 'But whatever it is, don't hurt them or punish them. They are good kids. Just let them go.'

Milo hung by the door struggling to free himself from the Disciplods' tight grip.

Pummelcrush laughed. 'You're too soft, Ursula. You always were. These kids are going to get what is coming to them. I will get my way. There's no turning back.' He turned to walk away. 'I'll decide what to do with you and this garden later. But I'd start packing. You're finished here.'

The group was led to the lift and brought down to the cave.

Pummelcrush called Gurney: 'Meet me in the lab. We need to accelerate our plans. Hurry!'

As the lift's steel doors opened, the group were led out into the cool air of the cave and marched down the tunnel. Their eyes scanned around trying to make sense of what was happening.

Unlike the others, Milo knew what was coming. He knew that they were about to be subjected to hours of virtual-reality torture and brainwashing. The image of Katie's eyes and her twitching body spasming as she lay helpless would be burned into his memory for ever.

Strong, questioning, open minds are the hardest to break. Strong, questioning, open minds are the hardest to break, he began to say to himself.

Then he started to repeat it out loud, getting his friends' attention.

'Everything can be questioned, and everything should be questioned. Do not accept things just because someone tells you to. Think for yourself.'

They were led down the tunnel towards the sign pointing to the lab.

And there it was, hanging from the centre of the ceiling, suspended like a sleeping executioner, waiting for its next chance to destroy lives: the REDUCON 6000.

Two StifleCorp engineers stood in the room talking with Gurney. Pummelcrush walked right over to them.

'Stop whatever you're doing,' he said. 'We have eight brats here, all guilty of heinous crimes against this school. If I had my way, they would be taken out and disposed of. But we can't do that these days. So, we do the next best thing: we remove their personalities, destroy their will, turn them into good, obedient students.'

'How would you like to proceed?' asked Gurney eagerly.

'We always intended for the REDUCON to process multiple students at once,' he said. 'Now it's time to see what this machine is capable of.' He rubbed the machine with his bony, wart-covered hand.

Milo could see the look on the engineers' faces: it was shock. They looked at Gurney in disbelief.

'Dr Pummelcrush,' said the older engineer, 'I'm not sure that's such a good idea. The machine is still in the testing stage. It's never been tried on more than one student at a time.'

'Silence!' snapped Pummelcrush. 'There is no time for indecision. The eyes of the world will be on the Institute in a matter of days and everything needs to be perfect. Get the headsets!'

'But, sir, this is madness,' the other engineer said. 'It's highly unlikely that the machine in its current state could process eight students with eight uniquely personalised virtual scenarios.'

'Highly unlikely, you say?' asked Pummelcrush.

'Yes, *highly* unlikely.'

'But possible?'

'It's not worth the risk. It's insanity!'

'I'll be the judge of that. Now. Go. Get. The. Headsets! If you talk back to me one more time, you'll never work for StifleCorp again! Disciplods, prepare the room.'

The Disciplods began strapping the students into the chairs.

The engineers returned, pushing a trolley full of shiny black headsets, just like the one Milo had seen lowered on to Katie's face – the pointed metal prongs, the smooth black visor.

Gurney was standing at the control panel with one of the engineers. 'Agnes, please, I'm begging you, this is unwise. Let's just give them a standard punishment: wait until after graduation and process them one at a time.'

Milo could see her blank stare: 'You heard what Dr Pummelcrush said. You have your orders.'

'Enough!' Pummelcrush snapped at the engineer. 'I am the genius who realised that it was the students who were the problem. I'm the one who saw that we needed to stamp out their will. I'm the one who thought of selling them for profit. I'm the one who created the perfect system that creates the perfect slave-workers. How dare you question me!'

'I want no part of this,' said one of the engineers, and she went to leave.

Pummelcrush grabbed her by the arm. 'You are going nowhere,' he snapped. 'Put the headsets on.'

Now Milo started to feel truly afraid. At the best of times, Pummelcrush was unhinged, but this marked a new level of crazy. He whispered to his classmates: 'Everyone, listen to me. Whatever happens, I want you to remember: strong, questioning, open minds are the hardest to break.'

'Shut up,' hissed Pummelcrush. 'Put on the mouth straps before I do something I regret!'

'No, I won't shut up!' answered Milo, now with nothing to lose. 'Sarah-Louise, Consuela, Liam, Gerry, Julia, everyone, we can get through this … just keep your minds open … don't be afraid of what you see. Whatever it is, it's not real. Be strong. Don't let fear close and narrow your mind. They want to make you afraid so you'll accept whatever they tell you.'

Milo kept talking about everything he could remember Ursula saying about philosophy. 'Strong, open, questioning minds are the hardest to break,' he said one last time before the Disciplod placed thick black tape across his mouth.

They attached a large steel-framed extender to the front of the REDUCON and then began connecting the headsets to the frame, using thick, heavy black cables.

Milo could see the panic and fear in his classmates' eyes, but also, he saw strength and resilience.

'Start the machine!' Pummelcrush commanded.

Milo stared at the engineers, pleading with his eyes. They saw him too. He could see them pausing, hoping there was some way out. But in the end, the engineer pushed a large red button.

The machine growled and whirred into action.

'Upload the Du-Ped file for each individual.'

Gurney began transferring the files for each student into the REDUCON 6000 database. Milo assumed this was so the REDUCON 6000 could create personalised sequences for each student based on their history, behaviour, grades, family members, likes and dislikes.

'Engage device; attach to visual field.'

The buzzing increased as the machine moved forward. The kids sat, powerless, awaiting their fate.

Just as it was approaching, Milo managed to loosen the tape across his mouth with his tongue: 'Remember,' he shouted, 'strong, open, questioning minds are the hardest to break! Strong, open, questioning minds –'

Pummelcrush rushed over and placed another piece of tape across Milo's mouth. The look in Pummelcrush's eyes was murderous.

'Set it to maximum strength! We will need every scrap of power it has.'

It began.

Milo braced himself. The two prongs inched closer and then pressed around his eyes, stretching them out so wide he thought they would fall out. It was excruciatingly painful.

Then a fine mist was sprayed. He desperately wanted to blink, to shut his eyes for a moment, but he couldn't.

The black visor closed tightly around his face, shoving his head right back against the chair, blocking out the lights and transporting him into pitch-black dimensionless space.

Then, in an instant, the chairs lifted into the air, stretching their bodies out wide.

Slowly, images and shapes began to emerge from the darkness. But it didn't feel like watching a screen. It felt like opening your eyes after a deep sleep.

First, he was in his classroom and the teacher was shouting: 'You are the worst student we've ever had!' He saw expressions of disgust and disappointment on his friends' faces. Even Sarah-Louise and Katie shook their heads in disdain.

It got nastier; people began throwing things. A voice was repeating: 'You are a failure. A nobody. You don't deserve to be here. Nobody likes you.'

Milo was stunned. All thoughts he had of questioning and staying strong drained out of his mind when he was confronted with one of his worst fears: complete rejection by his friends.

He really felt like this was happening now: the smells, the atmosphere, the sense of time. He realised he was sobbing.

An instantaneous flash of something gruesome – maggots infesting a dead animal carcass – appeared before his eyes as it transitioned to another scene. He saw his parents in Gurney's office rocking back and forth, crying and wailing.

They looked up at him. 'How could you do this to us,' his dad cried, 'after everything we've sacrificed?'

Milo hadn't seen his dad this upset in years. It was shocking. His mother looked like she had been crying for days.

Gurney held up a piece of paper. It said, 'Failure: will amount to nothing!'

When his parents saw this they erupted into further wails of grief.

Milo was in hell – a horrific, heart-breaking hell. He placed his hands over his ears and tried with all his might to remind himself this wasn't real. It was the school. It was their last-ditch effort to try to break him.

But his memory of before was so elusive, so slippery. Yet, way deep down in his cells, he fought. Buried below his conscious awareness, he remembered something: *Strong, open, questioning minds are the hardest to break.* He repeated it. It began to block out his parents' desperate cries.

This is not real, he said to himself. *My parents love me. What I see is not always to be believed.*

Then the scene dissolved into little pieces and another image of something revolting appeared for a split second: this time it was huge rats devouring a dead cat. Next thing he knew he was back in the convention hall. There was a large crowd. All the students were lined up, smiling, about to receive their certificates.

Again, the brutal imposing reality of the scene severed his memory of only seconds before. Students made their way to the stage and were greeted with tremendous applause.

And then it was Milo's turn. He was smiling and excited. As he took a step on the stage, everyone turned to look at him. He was alone with a single spotlight shining down from above. 'This year, for the first time in history, we have one absolute and complete failure: Milo Moloney.'

He turned his head to look at the screen behind, to see embarrassing photos of him: pulling silly faces, in his underpants, on the toilet, getting sick, crying like a baby.

He then looked down and saw he was wearing only his underpants on stage. Everyone started to laugh. He could hear them saying things like: 'What a joke! Pathetic. What a total loser.'

He saw his parents crying.

This was too much. He felt sick, nauseous and dizzy. All his worst fears were being used against him. He was disoriented and confused, and he blamed himself. He felt so small. He had shrunken down to the size of a tiny insect and was being shouted at by a universe of humungous adults who told him he was worthless.

But again, deep in his subconscious the line emerged: *Strong, open, questioning minds are the hardest to break.* He clung on to this thought to return slowly, back to his real memories. He remembered the garden, Ursula, his friends – and philosophy.

He told himself, *This is not real. I don't have to accept it. I can question it. I can think for myself.*

And he dearly hoped that his friends could do the same.

The scenes kept coming. Flashes of horrific imagery, followed by degrading and shameful situations. There was a flash forward into his future as a young man in his twenties being blocked from entering university, being rejected from everywhere he tried to get a job. Another showed him growing old, alone and poor, and all because he failed to submit and surrender to the system and follow orders like everyone else.

Milo kept fighting it. He repeated the mantra in his head: *Strong, open, questioning minds are the hardest to break.*

Then, out of nowhere, there was a jolt in the sequence. It was the strangest sensation, like as if reality itself froze and jumped, first fast-forward, then slow-motion, then blackout.

It shook Milo out of the heavy-headed state he had been in. Even though he had been fighting and questioning, all his senses were still telling him these scenes were real, and the mental strain was immense. This jolt was like a breath of fresh air.

Then the sequence of scenes kicked back in. A thousand social media posts all ridiculing Milo as a failure.

Another jolt. This time for slightly longer. *It's working,* he thought. *Keep questioning. Keep imagining. This is not how things have to be.*

Another jolt; followed by another.

Milo was becoming aware of his actual surroundings again. He hoped the others were also experiencing the cracks in the system. He started to hear a high-pitched buzz. He was sure it was different to the usual low, smooth hum of the REDUCON. He heard random cracks and bursts of sparks somewhere close by.

Now the sequences were a jumble of pixels.

'Sir, the system is reaching overdrive. It's breaking up!'

Milo smiled and his heart filled with strength.

'WHAT IS THE MEANING OF THIS?' Pummelcrush cried out.

The high-pitched buzzing rose in pitch and intensity.

BOOOOM! The screen went blank. The illusion was broken.

'You,' Pummelcrush growled to one of the engineers, 'get this back up and running this instant! They haven't had enough exposure time. Quickly, before it wears off and we have to start all over again.'

Milo and the others couldn't see, but they could hear. They heard the silence that followed Pummelcrush's order.

'Well?' Pummelcrush screamed. 'What are you waiting for, you absolute moron?'

'Sir, please, the internal processer is no longer functioning,' said the engineer. 'The processer couldn't handle that number of sequences simultaneously. But what's even more striking is the resistance levels.' Milo could hear relief in the engineer's voice.

'The what?'

'The resistance levels. How ready the mind is to accept what it is told by authority. In this case, the resistance levels were off the charts. That must be why the machine couldn't cope.'

'You're telling me that these pathetic idiots were somehow able to defeat the most advanced technology ever created!? Can we get it working again or not?'

'Perhaps, but it will take days. I've never seen anything like this before. From a pure research perspective, it's fascinating.'

'Arrrgghhh!' screamed Pummelcrush. 'I don't give a damn if it's *fascinating*. I need these children broken now. Get this fixed as fast as you can. In the meantime – lock them up in one of those cages. I'll tell their parents they are on some special project. Once the machine is fixed we can process them again.'

Silence.

'Do as I say!'

'Finnegus, I'm not so sure blatantly imprisoning children is the best way forward,' said Gurney cautiously.

'Oh, now you have some moral issues? You're fine with torture, brainwashing and selling them, but locking a few dirty brats up for a few days is a problem?'

There was no reply.

'You speak one more word back to me and I'll throw you in the cage with them. We have a goal and I'll be damned if I let anything get in my way!'

Milo was sure that Pummelcrush had completely lost it.

His headset was removed. He shielded his eyes from the blinding laboratory light. The tape was then ripped off his face. He stretched his mouth to encourage the blood back to his lips.

There, standing before him, untying his wrists, was his old friend Katie, her eyes blank.

The Disciplods grabbed Milo and the others, tossed them into a nearby cage and locked it. They left the lab along with Pummelcrush and Gurney. The last Disciplod switched off the lights as he shut the door.

Milo and his pals were alone. The only light came from the emergency exit sign over the door, a bluish hue making the young, traumatised faces barely visible.

Chapter 14

We are asleep. Our Life is a dream.
But we wake up sometimes,
just enough to know that we are dreaming.
– Ludwig Wittgenstein

Sarah-Louise hugged Milo. 'Are you OK?'

'Yes, I'm fine. A little dazed, but overall I'm not bad. And you?'

'Yes,' said Sarah-Louise. 'I'm all right. Oh, Milo, it was awful, though. I felt so bad, like a worthless piece of crap.'

'I know, same here. That's how it works, I guess. It grinds you down until you feel so low you will agree to anything to make it stop.'

'Do you think our philosophy conversations helped?' Sarah-Louise asked, as the others gathered around them.

'I think so. Every time I'd go into a deep hole, I'd pull myself up again by remembering to question.'

'Me too!'

Milo turned to the others. 'Is everyone OK?'

Consuela was squinting. Liam and Gerry were stretching their long arms, their big hands reaching high above them.

'Yes,' answered Julia. 'I'm just a bit shaken and confused.'

'We need to get out of here and stop Pummelcrush,' said Milo.

'Milo, we are stuck in a locked cage,' said Sarah-Louise. 'We can't do anything.'

'Euuughghhh!' Milo started kicking at the door of the cage.

'He can't keep us locked here for ever, right?' said Sarah-Louise. She kept looking at and fiddling with her smart-watch in that obsessive way of hers. 'Surely Ursula will help us. And when we do get out, we will take him down. This is plain evil. They can't get away with it.'

'But how?' asked Milo.

'Don't worry about that right now. Just trust me. I have an idea – if we can just get out of here.'

Milo smiled at his friend. He knew her idea would be good, whatever it was.

They all pushed and pulled the bars, kicked and screamed. But it was to no avail. They were trapped.

Eventually, one by one, they gave up and fell silent. They slumped on the ground, exhausted.

Then Milo spoke: 'That virtual-reality stuff was pretty weird, huh?'

'Big time!' Liam said.

'It was so real,' Consuela whispered.

'It was,' said Sarah-Louise. 'It was so hard to believe it wasn't real.'

'What if we were still in it?' asked Milo.

'What do you mean? It broke, didn't it?' Julia asked.

'Yes, I know. But think about it. What if it breaking and everything was all part of it ...'

'Stop, Milo, you're freaking me out,' said Consuela. 'Do you really think it is?'

'Well,' said Milo, 'how do we know what's real and what's not?'

GERRY: How do we know what's real and what's not? That seems like a question Ursula would ask us.

SARAH-LOUISE: We know that we are sitting here now talking. That I can see the cage door, and that I'm in a school and that Pummelcrush just left.

MILO: OK, but how can you be so sure that that's all true?

SARAH-LOUISE: Because I can see you, hear you, can feel the ground under my feet. It's obvious.

MILO: But weren't the sequences as real as that? Can you be absolutely sure that it is all exactly true?

CONSUELA: Yes, Milo. It's different now.

MILO: How?

CONSUELA: Well, because we don't have any visors on, we are not strapped in, and everything is consistent. It just makes sense.

MILO: So, you are saying you trust your senses – your eyes, your body, your ears. The information they give you is certain and trustworthy?

CONSUELA: Yes, I think so.

MILO: But was there ever a time when they misled you?

CONSUELA: Yeah, sometimes I think I see one thing, but it turns out to be another. But I still figure that out through my senses.

MILO: But we learned in science that things – things like tables and chairs – are really just piles of vibrating atoms. When we look through a microscope things look way different. And we know that dogs can hear sounds we can't hear, birds and bees can see things we can't see. So who really sees what's real? Do we just see what our senses let us see?'

CONSUELA: Hmm, I don't know.

MILO: Or what if all this is really a dream? And in reality you are just asleep in your bed?

GERRY: Really?

LIAM: Is that even possible?

SARAH-LOUISE: It's *possible* that this is a really long and realistic dream. But it doesn't seem like a dream. It seems real.

MILO: And how can you tell the difference?

SARAH-LOUISE: It's hard to explain, but dreams are really weird. Sometimes I can fly, or sometimes my teeth fall out. Things like that that never really happen when I'm awake. But the main reason is that I always wake up from dreams. And I never wake up from reality.

MILO: You mean you haven't woken up from reality yet ...

GERRY: Ahhh!

LIAM: Good point!

JULIA: As in, maybe reality is one long dream that we might wake up from?

MILO: Well, why not?

CONSUELA: No, but wait. If that's the case, then that wouldn't mean I don't know that we are here talking. It just means that we are here talking in a different place … and this is all a really long dream that has smaller sleep-dreams within it. This is still real.

MILO: Hmm, interesting. Yeah…So even if this is a dream, it's still real?

CONSUELA: Yeah, just a different *kind* of real.

MILO: OK, well then, what if it's a simulation? What if, in reality, we are all just bodies that are hooked up to machines that are making us *think* we are having these experiences, but it's all an illusion? Like one huge powerful REDUCON that never switches off.

JULIA: Yikes. If that were true, then I could never be sure that anything was real. Are you saying that might be true?

MILO: Not really, But it's possible, is all.

JULIA: What do you mean?

MILO: What if our reality, our entire universe, was a simulation created by more intelligent or advanced creatures?

GERRY: No way – how could that be?

MILO: Well, we don't have any really good answers for where our universe comes from, right?

GERRY: What about the Big Bang? That's what we learned in class. That there was a tiny, tiny dot and one day it expanded to create all the space and time and matter we see around us.

MILO: OK, yes. But, it doesn't answer the question: where did the tiny dot come from and what caused it to expand?

GERRY: What about God? Some people believe that God created the universe.

MILO: Yes, but where did God come from? Who created God?

GERRY: Well, maybe he or she always existed.

MILO: It's possible. But it seems hard to accept, doesn't it? That something just always existed for ever right back and never had a beginning? Surely things have to start somewhere.

CONSUELA: Hmm, yes, they do. But it has to be, doesn't it? Otherwise, if we say something else caused God or the Big Bang, then we have to say what caused that, and what caused that and so on for ever.

MILO: Right – a chain that goes back for ever – which is weird. I mean, I guess it's possible that something just came from nothing.

SARAH-LOUISE: How can something come from nothing? That's like a basic law of the universe isn't it?

MILO: Yeah, I think so. But if you want to accept that God was always there, or the universe was always there, why not accept that it just sprung into being from nothing? Both seem hard to accept.

LIAM: Weird. But a simulation, really?

MILO: Why not? We create simulations, don't we? With computer games and virtual reality. Imagine if in thousands of years they became so complex that they are almost like reality. Maybe that's happened already, thousands of years ago. We don't have any very easy answers as to where our universe came from, so maybe it is a simulation, created by some super-intelligent species, or even other humans.

CONSUELA: Would that mean our reality, our history, our lives, are not really real?

MILO: I don't think it would mean that. What we experience is real, I think; we just don't know where it comes from.

And on it went, the gang of prisoners, locked up below the supposed greatest school in the world, in the dark, discussing philosophy and the nature of reality while they awaited their fate.

Chapter 15

The most revolutionary thing one can do is
always to proclaim loudly what is happening.
— Rosa Luxemburg

'Milo, Milo, wake up!'

'Huh?'

'There's someone at the door,' Sarah-Louise whispered.

Milo opened his eyes. He could hear rustling near the door.

'What if it's Pummelcrush back to finish us off?' asked Consuela.

Milo stretched and rubbed his eyes. 'No, it couldn't be. It's graduation today. He'll be too busy.'

The door clicked open. A shaft of light appeared on the ground. They held their breath.

'Hello?' came a voice, hesitant and unsure.

Footsteps followed.

And then, a petite figure emerged from the dark.

'Ursula!' cried Milo, jumping up and grabbing the bars of the cage.

'I'm sorry it took so long,' said Ursula, matter-of-factly. 'I had to figure things out. Anyway, I sneaked into Agnes Gurney's office and stole her key-card.'

'And you didn't get caught?' asked Sarah-Louise.

'Oh, I still have a few tricks up my sleeve,' Ursula replied. 'It was easy. Everyone is so distracted by graduation. It's like a circus up there.'

'Nice job, Ursula! But now what do we do?' asked Milo.

'Let me just get you out of this awful cage first.' Ursula held the key-card up to the cage door. It beeped and opened, and the kids were able to file out, one by one.

'Thanks, Ursula!'

'You're a legend.'

They all stood around, stretching their arms and legs.

'Now what do we do?' asked someone.

'Well, we need to stop Pummelcrush,' said Milo.

'But how do we do that?' asked Ursula. 'No-one will believe us. He seems to have every angle covered – parents, politicians, probably the police.'

Everyone fell silent for a moment.

Then Sarah-Louise spoke up: 'I have a plan. First, we need to get out of here. Then, Milo, I need you – and you others, Ursula too – to go up to the convention hall and delay the ceremony for as long as you can. Disrupt it, buy me some time. I have to get things set up.'

'What kind of things?' asked Milo.

'I need to get to the control room of the convention hall.'

Milo stared at Sarah-Louise. He couldn't imagine what she had in mind. But he trusted her.

'Right,' said Ursula. 'Follow me.'

She led the gang out of the laboratory. She checked up and down the tunnel. Then they darted to the lift and went up. The doors opened on a desolate corridor.

The group of kids made their way towards the convention hall, checking around corners as they went. The odd drone-ball whizzed passed without detecting them. *Even the tech in this school is distracted*, thought Milo.

As they moved through the school, they could see rows of big black shiny cars parked outside. Some of the cars had those tiny flags on the front. They had to belong to the prime ministers and ambassadors of other countries. Set up across the immaculate lawns was a string of TV news vans and trucks with big logos on the side and satellite dishes on top. A long red carpet stretched out from the entrance of the school all the way down the avenue. Everything looked so perfect.

As they neared the convention hall, they heard pumping music coming from inside. Someone was on a microphone, ushering the crowd.

Sarah-Louise spoke: 'OK, this is where I leave you. Remember, just buy as much time as possible. Leave the rest to me. Julia, maybe you'd come with me?'

'I'll come too,' said Liam.

'And the rest of you, create a distraction in the hall. I need about five minutes, maybe a bit more.'

Ursula, Milo, Gerry and Consuela entered the hall quietly.

Pummelcrush's smooth, charming tone had returned. 'We would like to extend a special welcome to our guests of honour. We are very proud to have ministers of education from China, Japan, the USA, Australia, South Africa along with business leaders from the UK, France, Russia and Brazil. And, of course, our own Taoiseach. Today we hope to make history and become the greatest school that has ever existed.'

The audience rose to give a standing ovation. The camera crew turned their cameras from the stage to the room, trying to capture the atmosphere. The dignitaries and the executives whispered to each other and slapped each other on the back. There was a sense that the world was watching. That this was the place to be.

Pummelcrush gently raised his hands.

'I would like to welcome up a special guest, and a dear personal friend of mine, the CEO of StifleCorp: Penelope Clodfist.'

A small, round woman with glasses got up to speak to a warm round of applause. Milo recognised her from the night Katie got processed. The StifleCorp CEO waffled on. Another round of applause broke out as she finished her speech: 'And finally, once again, none of this would be possible without the educational genius, Dr Finnegus Pummelcrush.'

Pummelcrush strode back onto the stage as if he was a floating saint, a look of naïve confusion on his face that said: *Little old me?*

Penelope Clodfist went on: 'Dr Pummelcrush, I'm honoured to inform you that the Secondary Training Institute for Lifelong Employment is officially the highest-performing school of all time, and the number one ranked school in the world!'

Pummelcrush held his hands to his face and bent over, portraying the image of a humbled man genuinely surprised as the crowd roared. Multi-coloured streamers and confetti burst from the ceiling, as the music exploded into a cacophony of celebration.

'Milo, now!' whispered Ursula, and she started down the aisle towards the stage.

Milo wasn't sure what she wanted him to do, but he followed her. They had to distract the audience, as Sarah-Louise had asked. They would have to think of something.

'Please! Everyone listen!' Ursula shouted as the applause died down.

It took a minute for people to notice her small frame as she stood just below the stage. But slowly a hush descended.

'There is something you need to know,' Ursula said, speaking softly now, the microphones along the stage amplifying her voice.

Milo, standing just behind her, watched Pummelcrush as he tried with all his might to supress his rage. He nodded to his Disciplods, who were lined up along the sides of the room like military guards, and they got ready to move.

'This man,' Ursula said with a quiver in her voice, pointing to Pummelcrush, 'this man has not been educating your children – he has been torturing and brainwashing them! He has been creating an army of lifeless automatons capable only of following orders. And he has been selling them as slave-workers to corporations, including StifleCorp!'

Silence.

Ursula paused and looked around. Milo could see confused faces in the crowd looking at her as if she was some crazy lady who had wandered in off the streets. Only then did Milo notice how dishevelled they both were. Ursula was always so neatly turned out, but the last twenty-four hours had been stressful. Her hair was a mess, and there were patchy stains on her clothes. And he was filthy and bedraggled.

'Who the hell is this person?' a nearby parent whispered.

'This is highly embarrassing,' said someone else.

'Is this some kind of joke?' said another.

There were supressed giggles here and there.

'Get out of here, you nut job!' came a cry from deep within the crowd. 'You're ruining the ceremony!'

'Now, everyone,' said Pummelcrush, stepping forward, his voice smooth, 'please, let's show some kindness. This poor unfortunate lady is obviously experiencing some kind of mental breakdown.'

Milo watched as Pummelcrush read the mood of the room. He nodded to a Disciplod, who moved towards Ursula, accompanied by the Taoiseach's bodyguards.

'Stay back!' Milo shouted, jumping in front of Ursula. 'She's telling the truth. I'm a student here. And we were just caged up underneath the school after he tried to brainwash us!'

'Ah, yes,' said Pummelcrush, once again commanding the room, 'one of the very rare troubled students. Such a shame – but even we, the greatest school in the world, have our minor problems to work on!'

The crowd laughed a little and relaxed.

'I think we have had quite enough disruption today,' Pummelcrush said clinically. 'Please escort these two out and make sure they get the care they need.'

But before they were escorted out, Pummelcrush spoke again: 'Unless, of course, you have proof of these insane allegations?'

'Well, I don't know,' mumbled Milo, 'if you just wait, you'll see.'

'You have to believe us...' pleaded Ursula

'Well?' said Pummelcrush.

'It's just, if you just...' Milo turned to Ursula and whispered, 'Where the hell is Sarah-Louise?'

'Please,' Pummelcrush gestured again to the Disciplods and the security guards, 'take them out.'

'No, wait, you have to listen!' Milo pleaded with the crowd as he was being dragged away. 'He destroyed my friend Katie. He turned her into a zombie. They have a machine. It's virtual reality.'

Muffled giggles broke out among the crowd. People started to take out their phones to film the commotion. Milo could imagine the headlines: *Crazy old lady and disgruntled kid disrupt historic ceremony.*

He hung his head and gave up.

Ursula also stopped protesting.

They were just at the exit door when there was a loud crackle over the sound system, like the sound of a headphone jack being wriggled around in a speaker.

Milo pulled free of his Disciplod and turned back to Ursula.

The sound was indecipherable, just muffled voices and machinery.

'Look! The screen!' Milo yelled.

Just moments ago it had been playing a looped video about the glorious achievements of the Institute. But now, it was showing a laboratory, and standing in frame was Pummelcrush's unmistakable image, and an audio track was running:

> *Here's the situation,* he was saying. *We have eight brats here, all guilty of heinous crimes against this school. If I had my way, they would be taken out and disposed of. But we can't do that these days. So, we do the next best thing: we remove their personalities, destroy their will, turn them into good, obedient students.*
>
> *How would you like to proceed?*
>
> *We always intended for the REDUCON to process multiple students at once. Now it's time to see what this machine is capable of.*
>
> *Dr Pummelcrush, I'm not sure that's such a good idea. The machine is still in the testing stage. It's never been tried on more than one student at a time. It still has issues to be worked out.*
>
> *Silence! There is no time for indecision. The eyes of the world will be on the Institute in a matter of hours and everything needs to be perfect. Get the headsets!*

A stunned hush fell on the crowd.

Pummelcrush moved quickly to talk over the audio. 'Now, please, ladies and gentlemen, this is obviously some kind of elaborate set-up.'

But the audience shushed him.

Milo turned to Ursula. 'Sarah-Louise is a genius! *That's* why she was constantly fiddling with her smart-watch!'

'She recorded it!' said Ursula, amazed. 'She used the school's technology against itself! What a kid!'

Pummelcrush whispered to more Disciplods, who ran off stage.

But just as he did there was more:

> *I am the genius who realised that it was the students who were the problem. I'm the one who saw that we needed to stamp out their will. I'm the one who thought of selling them for profit. I'm the one who created the perfect system that creates the perfect slave-workers. How dare you question me!*

Milo could see everyone's faces drop.

Parents held their children close. Journalists scrambled between phone calls. Camera operators could hardly believe what they were capturing, live on air, broadcast across the world. *This is history all right*, thought Milo, *but not the version everyone was expecting to be written today.*

The room descended into chaos. Parents started shouting.

'Keep that monster away from my children!'

'I knew this place was too good to be true.'

'I'm calling the police.'

Many of the dignitaries, including the StifleCorp CEO, the Taoiseach and the international ministers of education, made hurried exits, wishing to avoid an awkward PR moment. But it was too late. The truth was out, and it was unavoidable.

The shouting continued as Pummelcrush desperately searched the room, looking for a way out. For the first time, he looked lost, like a frightened rabbit in headlights.

Then he locked eyes with Milo. That hateful stare returned to his eyes, and, without warning, he leaped off the stage, pulled his electrified baton from his pocket and lunged at Milo. His bony hand was clawing at the air as the buzzing baton came down upon Milo.

Pummelcrush's eyes had the look of blind, psychopathic rage.

But just as he was about to get a hold of Milo, Gerry and Consuela jumped on him and tackled him to the ground. They were followed quickly by two massive bodyguards standing nearby.

Just then, the two Disciplods emerged from behind the stage holding a squirming Sarah-Louise.

'Get your hands off her!' shouted Milo. 'It's over. Let her go!'

The two Disciplods, seeing their master on the ground, ran to his side. Milo pitied them. They were discombobulated – years without thinking for themselves had rendered them incapable of adapting to unexpected situations. They dropped to their knees and held their hands over their ears to block out the shouting and chaos.

Milo hugged Sarah-Louise tightly: 'You're amazing. How did you think of recording it! You played it just in time!'

She hugged him too. 'Milo,' she said, 'I just hope we can bring Katie back.'

'Me too.'

The police showed up soon afterwards and began taking statements, investigating the caves below and making arrests; Gurney, Clodfist and Pummelcrush were the first to be bundled into the police car.

Milo's parents arrived.

'Milo, are you OK?' his mam asked, checking him from head to toe, licking her thumb to clean his dirty face, but then hugging him instead. 'We got here as soon as we saw what was happening. We were watching it live.'

'Milo, we are so sorry,' his dad said. 'We just ... we feel awful. You told us and we didn't listen. We are so, so sorry.'

'Well,' said Milo, 'I'll forgive you,' stretching it out for as long as he could, 'only if you do what you are told from now on.'

They laughed and hugged him again.

Milo spotted Ursula approaching. He introduced her to his parents, but just as he did so, there was a rush as all the reporters moved towards her.

'Ursula Joy, how did you find out?' The questions came thick and fast. 'How long have you known?'

Ursula looked at Milo and smiled, cleared her throat and waited for silence. Then she spoke, softly this time: 'I will give one statement. And then you must leave here and allow us time to help these children and young adults recover.'

The crowd of bustling reporters calmed.

'We now know that the Secondary Training Institute for Lifelong Employment has been designed with one purpose: to turn bright, hopeful students into dull, lifeless slaves. It's easy for us to blame Dr Pummelcrush. It's easy to blame

StifleCorp and call them evil. But the truth is, we are all to blame. Parents, teachers, politicians, the media; all of us bought into the myth of the Institute. All of us cheered when the school climbed those rankings. We didn't care what it was doing to our children. They warned us. But we didn't believe them. We didn't listen to them. We blindly trusted in a powerful institution because we thought they could do no wrong. We failed to think for ourselves. We failed to question what was going on here. And so now we must face up to that fact and ask ourselves: why *do* we educate children? And how do we educate children? Is it just to climb rankings? Is it to create workers who will slave away night and day? Well, I say *no* to that. I say that we educate to create independent, imaginative, curious, compassionate, creative children, who are able to think for themselves. Our children are not some resource to be shaped and moulded for profit. So please, leave us now to rebuild this school, maybe not as the number one ranked school in the world, but as a place where children will learn to open their minds, question the ideas they receive and develop an ability to imagine a new and better world.'

She stopped and smiled at Milo.

'Excuse me,' she said, and she left the room with dignity and grace, her head held high.

Chapter 16

The philosophers have only interpreted the world,
in various ways. The point, however, is to change it.
— Karl Marx

The next few days were a whirlwind. This was massive news, a huge scandal. The police found connections to nearly every country in the world. Videos and pictures of the event itself – of Pummelcrush leaping off the stage with an electrified baton to attack a child after being caught in a torture and brainwashing operation – spread like wildfire across the internet, TV and all the newspapers.

Milo, Ursula, Sarah-Louise and the others were at the centre of the media attention. Every reporter and news station desperately wanted to talk to them and were willing to pay big money for exclusive interview rights. But Ursula refused almost every one. She wouldn't let them talk to her students. She gave a small number of interviews herself, just to set the record straight. But she refused to allow the media get their grubby claws into her young friends, even if they were billed as child-heroes.

The friends didn't care much about the attention or the celebrity. That is not to say they didn't enjoy the praise and adulation, and most especially the feeling of finally being proven right. But really, only one thing mattered to them. And while they were distracted in the immediate days afterwards, there was only one thought they kept returning to: how could they find a way to bring Katie and the others back to themselves?

The children who had been brainwashed were taken to hospital for testing, including Katie and Paul Patrick. They were examined, but, to Milo and Ursula's shock, they were released after a few days. The doctors ran all the tests they could: bloods, respiratory, eyes, ears, fitness, heart rate, blood pressure and so on. They found all the kids to be in perfect physical health.

But while they were physically healthy – no doubt thanks to the daily nutri-paste – there is no denying they were shells of their former selves.

Milo and Sarah-Louise spent several nights at Katie's house trying to coax her back with fun, games and movie nights. But after a week, she was still the same. Several times they found her in her pyjamas in the middle of the night walking to the Institute, mumbling about how it was the greatest school ever created.

Milo and Sarah-Louise went to meet Ursula soon afterwards to formulate a plan.

'What are we going to do?' asked Milo. 'I thought the impact of the brainwashing would wear off after a few days.'

'Yeah, me too,' said Sarah-Louise.

'I know, it's worrying,' said Ursula. 'But have faith. I have been meeting with a team of counsellors and psychologists. Together we are developing a recovery programme.'

'How does that work?' asked Milo.

'Remember when the machine broke, and they said the resistance levels were off the charts? Well, the programme is built around philosophical conversations, but supplemented with weekly therapy and support from the counsellors.'

'I miss Katie so much,' said Sarah-Louise, 'and I feel so guilty. I should have stayed with you guys that time in the corridor.'

'If anyone should feel guilty it's me,' said Milo. 'I was the one who couldn't wait. I had to run off and find out.'

'If we want to help Katie and Paul Patrick and all the others,' said Ursula, calmly and matter-of-factly, 'then we must first help ourselves. And that means we must forgive ourselves. Let the guilt and shame go. I mean it. It's essential. We all did what we thought was best at the time. And we simply do not know what would have happened had we done otherwise. We are here now. And we must be kind to ourselves to create the space to be kind to others. Do you understand me, Milo, Sarah-Louise?' Ursula looked into their eyes. 'Plus,' she continued, 'I am going to need your help with this programme.'

'You are?'

'Of course. Daily philosophical conversations are part of the recovery programme. It won't be easy, but I have faith that, alongside the support of the counsellors, these kids will find their way back. It takes a lot to destroy a human spirit.'

It would be a long, hard road, but they were ready for the challenge to help their friends.

It was decided that Ursula would take over the Institute as interim principal while they figured out what to do.

As it turned out, their little philosophy resistance squad became quite popular. Lots of people wanted to join them, some because they found the questions interesting, others so they could be protected against this happening ever again.

In the meantime, the friends were quite happy to hang out in the garden, listen to music and talk about the universe and everything else.

As for Clodfist, Gurney and the esteemed Dr Finnegus Pummelcrush – they're being forced to do community service while awaiting trial. You might spot them wearing high-vis jackets in the marshy gunk along the River Suir in Waterford, knee deep in stinking sewage and dirt, picking up rubbish.

Rumour has it that Pummelcrush can't stop roaring and screaming orders at Gurney and Clodfist, even though he has no authority, and is attending an anger-management course. As we know, some habits, like some spirits, are hard to break.

Acknowledgements

The idea for this book, and the writing of it, would not have been possible without the help of my family, friends and colleagues, and I wish to sincerely thank them for their support.

First and foremost, to my brother Andrew for his ideas, support, extreme patience and for helping me with most aspects of the book, from start to finish. To my other brother, Stephen, and my parents, Michael and Sheila, for their ideas, constant encouragement, love and support.

To my friends for listening to my notions, reading drafts, giving thoughtful feedback and for general support and soundness: Stephen Murphy, Philip Christie, Liam Ryan, Finnian Kelly, Ailbhe Forde, Brian Larkin, Chris Rooney, Della Kilroy, Leon Murphy, Peter Power, Eoin O'Herlihy, Risteard de Paor, Ross O'Neill, Sarah Hogan and, of course, big Ben Grant.

To Miriam Dignam, principal of St Kevin's GNS, and Mrs Forde's sixth class in St Kevin's GNS for allowing me to explore, learn and develop philosophical dialogues with them and for being so welcoming and kind.

To my friends and colleagues in the philosophy world for their work, support and for being a constant source of inspiration.

To John Bisset and Lynn Ruane, my Philosophy in the Community colleagues, for working with me to bring philosophical dialogue into places it wouldn't normally exist and for their tireless work in helping people who need it.

To Aislinn O'Donnell for being a mentor, a friend and always supporting me in doing philosophy outside the academy, from prisons to schools and everywhere in between.

To Jim, Dannielle, Tony, Niall, Kate, Anne, Ger, Noreen, Trish, Karl, Tony, Colm, Chris, Mary, Eilish, Ciara, Stuart, Ciaran and everyone from the Rialto philosophical dialogue groups and in St Andrew's Community Centre for all the thoughts, ideas and conversations, and the listening, openness and presence.

To Austin O'Carroll and the 'Bang Bang' philosophy group for the philosophical conversations and discussions.

To Anne Costelloe, June Edwards and Paula Egan for allowing myself, Elizabeth Meade and Sabrina Keenan to do philosophy in Mountjoy Prison, and to all the groups who came and talked philosophy with us.

To Susan Andrews, Marelle Rice, Áine Mahon, Gillen Motherway, Gerry Dunne, Charlotte Blease and all the Philosophy Ireland crew for their help and inspiration in promoting philosophy in schools and the wider community.

To Alan Gilsenan, Martin Mahon and Oliver Fallen for helping me spread the word about philosophy.

To Stomptown, The Bonk and Our European Partners for all the musical, creative and craic-based times.

To Gráinne Clear for having the original idea for me to write a philosophy book for children. To Síne Quinn, who took my manuscript and transformed it into something real and readable. And to Siobhán Parkinson and Matthew Parkinson-Bennett for their insight, patience and kindness in the process of getting this book finished and out into the world.

We hope you have enjoyed reading *The Philosophy Resistance Squad*. On the following pages you will find out about some other Little Island books you might like to read.

Little Island

WOLFSTONGUE

By Sam Thompson

Illustrated by Anna Tromop

Deep in the Forest, the foxes live in an underground city built by their wolf slaves. The foxes' leader Reynard controls everything with his clever talk.

At school, Silas is getting bullied because his words will not come. He wishes he could live in silence as animals do.

Then Silas meets an injured wolf and helps him. Isengrim, Hersent and their pups are the only wolves left, moving between the human and animal worlds using hidden passageways as they fight to survive.

When Silas enters the secret world of the Forest he will learn that, even here, language is power. Can he find his voice in time to help his wolf friends – can he become the Wolfstongue?

'An edge-of-the-seat adventure.' – Meg Rosoff

'An unforgettable fable.' – Lucy Strange

'A highly original story, warm and thoughtful, full of insight.'
– Kelly McCaughrain

'Heartwarming and brave.' – Myra Zepf

'Wolfstongue has modern classic written all over it.' – Patricia Forde

THE WORDSMITH
By Patricia Forde

Letta loves her job as the Wordsmith's apprentice, giving out words to people who need them. It doesn't strike her as odd that the people of Ark are only allowed to use a few hundred words, and words like 'love', 'hope' and 'freedom' are banned.

When her master disappears, Letta starts to understand that all is not well – John Noa, the ruler of Ark, is out to destroy language altogether. Letta has to find a way to stop him silencing what is left of the human race.

But she's only a young girl, and he's the leader of the known world...

'The fantasy book of the year.' – Eoin Colfer

'A novel that truly stands apart for its originality and relevance... a book about words, about language, about their power to civilise – and, in the wrong hands, to abuse and dehumanise.' – *The Irish Times*

WINNER OF A WHITE RAVEN AWARD FROM THE INTERNATIONAL YOUTH LIBRARY

MOTHER TONGUE

By Patricia Forde

The sequel to *The Wordsmith*

After Global Warming came The Melting. Then came Ark.

Letta is the wordsmith, tasked with keeping words alive. Out in the woods, she and the rebels secretly teach children language, music and art.

Now there are rumours that babies are going missing. When Letta makes a horrifying discovery, she has to find a way to save the children of Ark – even if it is at the cost of her own life.

'Subtle, humane and inspiring. An amazing book.'
– Anne Booth, author of *Across the Divide*

'Totally enthralling … a world where the horror of climate change has been realised but despite the despair, the hope of humanity lives on.'
– *The Book Activist*

About the Author

Robert Grant was born in Waterford. He has a PhD in philosophy from Trinity College Dublin, where he was an Irish Research Scholar. He has taught philosophy both at Trinity and in several other institutions. Rob is founder of the Philosophy in the Community project and a member of Philosophy Ireland, and has taught philosophy in schools, prisons, community centres and many other places. He has written and talked about this work for *The Irish Times*, RTÉ radio and television, BBC radio, Newstalk radio and many other places. He lives in Dublin, but is still from Waterford.

About Little Island

Founded in 2010 in Dublin, Ireland, Little Island Books publishes good books for young minds, from toddlers all the way up to older teens. In 2019 Little Island won a Small Press of the Year award at the British Book Awards. As well as publishing a lot of new Irish writers and illustrators, Little Island publishes books in translation from around the world.

www.littleisland.ie